ONE FROM THE ICE

One From the Ice

Stories by Sean Welsh

Eclectic Press, inc.

This book is a work of fiction. Names, characters, places, and incidents are the product of the author's imagination or are used fictitiously. Any resemblance to actual events, locales, or persons, living or dead, is coincidental.

Copyright © 2010 by Sean Welsh all rights reserved. No part of the contents of this book may be reproduced, stored in a retrieval system, or transmitted in any form or by any means, electronic, mechanical, photocopying, recording, or otherwise without written permission of the publisher.

First published in 2010 by Eclectic Press by arrangement with the author.

Eclectic Press, Inc.
P.O. Box 22
New York, NY 10159-0022
eclecticpress@gmail.com
Visit our website at www.eclecticpress.org

Edited by Charles Muller
Design and layout copyright © 2010 Eclectic Press, Inc.
Cover Design: Allan Linder
Produced by Eclectic Press, Inc.
Printed and bound by LuLu Publishing in the USA
Catalog records for this book are available from the Library of Congress.
ISBN 978-0-557-79858-2 (paperback edition)
1 2 3 4 5 6 7 8 9 10

To my parents Anne and Chris, and to all parents who have children that run in the night.

~ Sean Welsh

FOREWORD

New York is a place of change and struggle. Most people just call it progress. I was there for the change from a local burrito joint to a local pub. Construction took a few months before the grand opening. That's where I met Sean. He served up stories and cold beer, and I shared sketches and ideas. If you aren't prepared for change it's probably better to live somewhere else where change happens a little slower. As odd as it seems, New York is also a city of trust. It may take some time, but once trust is established, you can forge life long bonds.

Regardless of how much money you have in your bank account or how important you think you are, the most valuable tool you will ever have is imagination. Sean has plenty of it. After a year or two of developing trust, Sean was working on a story, and I was working on a new series of paintings. The seed of imagination was planted to create collaboration of art and literature.

Sean came over to my loft ready to work, carrying the necessary stock for my bar, and a fist full of ideas. He painted on steel, hammered on metal, applied found objects, and began to create a series of works that we would both remember as one of the best creative ideas we have ever had. The imagination that came out of that room was truly a creative force. Since then we have both seen many changes. Sean has managed to capture short moments in time, which I haven't seen since Franny and Zooey. It's the small things that separate a great artist from the rest of the population, little details that ordinary people forget, or overlook. Sean Welsh gets every detail with One From The Ice. His talent shines in his first book. I know you will enjoy this work of short stories as much as I did. Grab a cold one, turn off your TV and use your imagination!

~ *Allan Linder*, Artist, Author, Sculptor

TABLE OF CONTENTS

238TH STREET ———————————————— Page 7

A KNIFE IN THE SNOW ———————————— Page 16

FAITH AND SUNDAY ————————————— Page 25

SAUTÉED ON THE SHORE ————————————— Page 40

THE PORCH ————————————————— Page 50

THE QUIET MORNING ————————————— Page 64

THE TANK ————————————————— Page 74

UNCLE TOM'S SAAB —————————————— Page 103

WARM AND DRY ——————————————— Page 112

CUSTOMS ————————————————— Page 122

CHECKMATE ————————————————— Page 132

Sean Welsh

238TH STREET

He was late getting to the tunnel of the foyer. I stood, as pissed off as always, maybe a little more this time because I knew his reason for being late was not something unavoidable, but he was late anyway cause he knew it would piss me off.

A little cleaner, the foyer, just as hot with no toys or half stitched mitts, worn red softball bats, bent badminton rackets or an occasionally chewed ball from some sport, pulled by somebody's dog from some neighbor's Pac-of-Sandra. It had all been replaced by bargain priced replica vases to match the carpet. The perennial cracked stucco was smoothed over by dry wall and high gloss paint, beige ridden, sweating just as much as I was, still waiting.

"Don't they teach you to be on time?" I asked as he flung and closed the oak stained door brushing by, his blackened dirty glove tucked close to his chest.

"Let's go."

He slid through the white door with a deeper muffle than its previous aluminum out over the same lawn. We were allowed to run over it now that the ole man was dead. Strangely enough for all the hours the

One From The Ice

ole man put into the plush green forbidden space, it seemingly looked better after his death, and nobody could figure out why.

Driveway to driveway was still the same as I followed by thirty feet. The softer day's rays hit just the tips of the lawn, the remaining spray left by the arcing sprinkler painted my ankles, and I felt like goddamn Paul O'Neill as I started to jog heavy to the diamond of asphalt between the curbs, just as I newly felt years ago as goddamn

Donny Baseball.

His steps were just the same, quick and beautiful, though with more intensity. The only reason I knew that was how fast he covered ground. Tossing the ball to himself high, then behind his back, he let a car go by and then lobbed a lazy full throw that landed with a sprinkle of dust on the heel of "Schmidt" as I caught up.

"Been runnin'?" I said throwing timid.

"Have to," he said, throwing a dip that pocketed into my web.

"It shows." I launched a ball high that tore through some leaves, caught a tip of wind then landed into his gulch.

He took the ball and bit it. He smelled it and turned it over in his hands like silk in a dryer, smoother. The stir of stitch, leather, and skin carried distinctly, and I couldn't wait for him to do anything with it, but then he moved almost to the curb, then I, and a car went by.

"That's the Schmidt?" He whipped a shortstop side arm that stung my palm to the side of my face, and I was surprised that I caught it.

"Yeah," I said holding the ball fragile, letting it absorb the sweat that was seeping through slick. A little more wind kicked up so I kept my throw waist high and tight. My shoulder objected.

"You been playin'?" he asked with interest.

"Little. You?"

"Everyday." He banked a grounder off the curb that went high like a bad bunt. I charged it bare handed and threw it two feet over his head, sending him on the run.

"My bad," I said watching him sprint.

"Fuck you!" he yelled back catching up to the ball.

"Hard hittin' Mark Whitten!" He turned three driveways from his original spot and launched a prayer that I stepped two feet of the tree to meet.

"Should work on your arm!" I yelled waiting for him to get back.

"Fuck you," he said galloping, looking at the houses to his left.

One From The Ice

His face was gaunt, chiseled, wrapped with a tight brown beard, and there were some wrinkles around the corner of his eyes. His green eyes were the same, the same as when we were ten, the same as when we won state championships as seniors. His calves were thicker, his arms were thicker, and his stomach tighter, and I knew I couldn't do anything about the fact that he could kick my ass. I wondered about him drinking.

"You still drinking?" he asked.

"Yeah."

"I bet I put you under."

"Fuck you," I said because the truth hurt.

He threw a filthy pop that I had to jump for, surprisingly coming down within a cone. I lobbed it back proud.

"Why don't uh, why don't you move back a few feet." He glanced at me brushing his Nikes across loose asphalt I'm sure he wished was dirt.

"S'matter, the ole ego needs a session?" I said grinning, doing as he asked because I felt that way too.

"Fuck you," he motioned smiling.

A brown Caprice wagon strolled by doing the speed limit, then we stepped to the middle of the street with the rows of houses standing, cheering.

He curbed me another grounder I got in front of with a clean exchange and charging towards him, rifled it into his stretched black glove. "POP." He smiled. I jogged back to my spot.

A snap of thirty feet went up into the tree that shielded it from the sun. I dug in by sound only, catching a glimpse, wavering under it, coming up with it. Luck. I looked at him smiling, he had his back turned looking off.

"Tough guy!" He turned open gloved; I fired it in without a flinch. My shoulder objected.

"Surprised you fielded that last one," he said confidently.

I didn't say anything. I kept watching him slow and effortless. The ball would hit my glove, the ball would hit his, two and a half driveways away until there was a rhythm with the help of no cars.

He paused a moment, then shot one over my head. He did it on purpose I know, because I saw his arm release high, and not follow through. I shot after it surprised at the quickness of my reaction. I coned it four driveways up right before a sewer, launching a high lazy arc he had

One From The Ice

to move up for just past the tree. I jogged back heavy, my thighs tight, and nauseous spit caught in my throat. I barely caught his next throw, barely threw it back.

"You gotta quit smoking when you drink," he said holding the ball. "That's the key, don't smoke."

I put my glove out and he lasered one in that stung my palm sweet. I smiled rifling back; my shoulder objected. He got on the balls of his feet. I dug into the pavement. We set up a good rhythm with the wind through the leaves. The sun went deeper into night. We were getting good and dirty. Back and forth, glove to glove, on lawns deep in the hole, off curbs of second bases turning two, on bloodied knees to get 'em at first, behind the back, "stone skips" because there was no other choice. Long from the sewer to get 'em at home, Willie Mays bucket scoops that "Skipper" would rape us for but got the crowd to their feet. An old man was smoking a pipe on the stoop where the Plohetzki's used to live, and sometimes he would clap, and sometimes he would object, but he would never interfere. We went on, unconscious of anything but the sun, and that was only due to the fact that we needed it to some degree. As it went further down, we moved in closer.

Everything became an outline of gray, and the rainbow sherbet sun did not even peek through the spaces between the houses. The rapid fire symphony lulled, spawning slow leisure with intricately timed crotch grabs and spit. I was pissed I forgot the gum.

"Hey did you bring…"

"No, shut up," I said spitting an eloquent bomb to the ground.

He shook his head and threw the ball barely winded. He was in fantastic shape. I could tell because I was not. I was not going to let the level suffer though; I was not going to let him down.

"Shoulder hurt yet?"

"No."

"Fuckin' things gotta be jell-o by now."

"It's not, throw the goddamn ball."

He did, right at my head. I ducked and caught it. I threw a decent one back. My shoulder could not even object it was so numb, and I was glad, not even thinking about the next week and a half where I would not be able to move it.

"Let's finish strong," I said.

Dusk became a thing of the past, and I could see across passing cars with their lights on. The blood that was dripping from my knees and

One From The Ice

side of my thigh was dried, and I was ready to rip it all open again. I did. I ate asphalt. He ate asphalt.

"C'mon motherfucker!" I rang out.

Gold lights went on in the houses. There was some minor relief with the click and buzz of the streetlights. My kidney hurt with deep breaths, and I could not fully see him, just the outline of him, but I caught every one of his throws, and he mine. I gave as good as I caught so I would not disappoint him. I could not feel my right arm, my mouth was dry, and I was gagging. But he could not see that. I knew because he did not say anything.

No more spit, no more pauses, no more light, no cars, no thought but to catch and throw. Catch and throw. Catch and throw. He had to call it. I was not going to let him down. *Catch and throw*, I thought gagging, hating myself for forgetting the gum. Fuck it.

"Hey," he said holding up. I could barely move so I stood hunched.

"I got to get up early tomorrow."

"Yeah. What time do you ship out?"

"O-five hundred."

"Right."

"Let's go eat."

"Right," I said hobbling towards the house. I hoped I did not let him down. I would have played forever.

A KNIFE IN THE SNOW

The last time I remember feeling this good about a snowfall I was sober and seventeen on the linoleum of my parents house sprawled out and content to be alone for a while. I could barely get alone time in that house; there were a lot of us. Some music was on, I can't say what, and the refrigerator would hum in sporadic moments, but everything else was dead. I just decided to lay there and look out the window directly above the sink, and in the upper left corner of that window was a single flood light that highlighted that portion of the driveway by the side door, and falling all over that single light was snow coming down too fast and thick for the heat of the bulb to melt it. It just kept coming.

Pat was closing The Tavern early in wanting to get back to Woodlawn before the roads got really bad. He apologized, gave me a shot of Beam, and sent me out into the snow. I stood next to the gyro cart zipping up. It was the first time I felt New York dormant and dense, let alone completely white.

"Don't you ever close, man?" I asked walking by.

"No boss. Never close." He flipped kebobs and stomped his feet. Small piles of onion and chicken were moved to the corner of his griddle waiting, and small icicles started to form on the tips of his black mustache.

I was warm inside, and there was barely any wind as I turned to walk up the middle of 31st Street towards 36th Avenue. The chop shops and garages were not visible, and every car that aligned both sides of the street was buried to the roof by discarded snow thrown from the plows. Not even the criminals were out, and I was still thirsty.

"3:17." I huffed.

Back in Kansas City I would have been defrosting a junker trying to hook up an after hours in a parking lot with nobody I knew. Walking under the N train was better. In fact leaving where I lived to come to New York was better. It was not rushed; it was not desperate, or at least not as desperate as it used to be, as what had become the norm.

Everyone I had lied to for so many years was glad to see me go. All my friends that really were or pretended to be shook my hand and gave me a nice party. All the women to whom I told pretty things showed up to tell me to fuck off, and a couple of them just to fuck me. I only loved twice in K.C. and when I left, I left a long lady who was good to me

One From The Ice

on all fronts for several years. But she understood, and it helped that we were not in love.

I thought about that apartment with no electricity, no phone, and a dead man's smell seeping from the fridge and off the mildew in the shower. That poor fucker I put into the hospital, but he had a knife so fuck him. Paul the bartender who never bought me a drink, but looking back I never deserved one, and so under the shoulders of the N train was better, and I didn't know anyone which was fine.

It was better than taking rolled coins for forty ounces of Crazy Horse in thinking that I was living desperate, out there, feeling life all under the cozy umbrella of parents and friends trying to shield me from the shame and criticism that they knew would bury me. It was better than any writhing desperation I had for a woman. The nonsensical humiliation of failure seemed to hold no present and short sometimes-brilliant flashes of the past, but nothing more. It all rolled itself coupling with the depletion of two respectable influences that did not trust me anymore, and looked at me with two sets of strangers' eyes instead of a son as they once did. That sharp biting reality of everyday cascaded through family's eyes eroded with time, and ended hopefully with me here, walking in New York by myself…expecting nothing.

It was hard to be comfortable with no phone or electricity though not impossible. I did it so long I managed to find real peace in some moments, usually right at dusk. The only one not worried for me was me.

I learned that there were basics that I wanted that people could not, would not give me, and one I found I craved the most was respect. The others were a phone, food, and electricity. I always found a way for drink. Later on when I was evicted, I made sure I would not let my friend down in any of these areas when he asked me to join him in his first apartment outside of his graduation from college. He had a big heart and pity that he disguised as a legitimate need for a roommate.

I thought of my first months in New York. I thought of how they were filled with expectations and newfound history. Some nights I remembered how worrying would keep me up as I lay on the floor listening to the N train go back and forth as I looked up at the white lights of the Citibank building. Thoughts of how anger helped me to carry out the decision to leave in a controlled defiance, and how I felt my skin of old being shed with every new hand that I shook, and every street that I walked with a new humble confidence, finding solace in all of its anonymity.

I could drink as much as I wanted as long as the bills were paid and rent was covered. As long as there was bail money and some kind of

One From The Ice

rainy day "broken ribs" fund. Maybe I could start it tonight in New York, God bless the fuckin' possibilities with snow burying everything and the history of those you could get behind. The snow kept coming and I kept walking almost to 36th Avenue. My feet were wet, and I felt shameless knowing exactly where to go. It was not where I came from; it was not where I was living, it was now. I stood in front of McGivney's with frozen snot to wipe while I contemplated it all. The N train slid past shaking snow. I had a good enough amount to drink with, and I was still thirsty.

"LET THIS NIGHT STAND MOTHERFUCKERS!!!" was what I heard as I stomped snow off through the door. To my left was an older woman with a bronze drink and a brazen face with slightly red highlights at the top of her cheeks and throughout her nose. She smiled at me and slurred. There were a couple of small Latinos in the corner drinking Coronas, everything else was fogged, except for the bar and a stool. Nobody seemed unhappy to see a stranger, and the jukebox was playing loud without the care of neighbors, which opened things up for everybody. It sounded like Tony Bennett, definitely not Frank or one of the other crooners.

"WE'RE NOT LEAVIN' TILL THE PLOWS GO HOME!!!"

He finished shouting and stood in front of the opened end of the bar. Six something in a damp grey sweatshirt with a Michelob Light in one hand, balancing a cigarette with a long tired ash that led to a short glass that shifted with a cherry swimming in a deep mahogany liquid. He looked at me, past me, and then took a sip of his beer.

"Whatya have 'dhere kid?" the barman asked.

"Draft of Coors."

He hobbled away and smiled at the room not looking straight at anyone. A pear colored fluorescent light colored him brighter than anything else in the room, and he moved with absolutely no urgency or irritation, and as I looked around I noticed everyone had a drink.

The space he moved between was flanked by union stickers, pictures of people who had died, trophies of stuffed squirrel, a deer from the late sixties, and a couple for bowling and softball at the far end covered in dust, all surrounding the mighty cash register that was manual and silver, shiny and dimly lit by a clip on M.G.D. light probably from when the beer first was introduced. The taps were sunken under the bar on the other side, and I preferred not to see what was surrounding them.

"God bleshya, huney. Where you frum?" She slid into me spilling half her drink and her nasty all night cigarette breath. Her hair was typical brown and in a pony tail, and as I slid back to catch some semi

One From The Ice

decent air, I could not help but notice that she must have been good looking at one point.

"I live across the street," I said.

"Ohh, that's niiice." She swayed back and then in close, so the sides of her breast were rubbing my arm.

"My name's Joann." She put out her hand smiling to reveal a crowded city of teeth all bunched.

"Dave." I said.

"Hey!!! Jo Jo. Jo ma, Jo Jo dancer, Jo ma marina!!! Come take me to the corner." He didn't acknowledge me and took her other hand. He looked like he could have been prosperous or attractive at one time, and as he brushed past me and led her to the corner of the bar by the only window I could smell that he hadn't washed his black suit for days. I knew that smell, because I used to not wash my clothes for days. It was a stench between dried natural body fluids combined with everything else the garment caught from the air.

"Yu's had a good night 'er what?" The bartender appeared in front of me sipping from a Dunkin Donuts cup that looked two days old.

"Yeah. Not bad." I said.

"I seen yuh in here last week. Was your name?"

"Dave."

"Davey Boy, Paul. Nice ta meet ya's." He extended a hand and when I took it I noticed it did not feel right, and when he pulled it back to take another sip I noticed that he was missing the tops of his pinky and ring fingers. He had hair like Pete Rose and slightly tinted glasses that were encased by silver breadbox frames. He would adjust them after almost hacking up his innards, and just before lighting a long Parliament.

My beer went down, and Paul brought me another. I downed another, and Paul refilled it. I put another twenty on the bar and Paul gave me one on the house. The bottles stood like soldiers with the best ones clean and often used, a lot of whiskey soldiers, and a lot of their fans waiting in exquisite swollen worship. Paul rolled the machine quiet and efficient, sometimes pretending to laugh through clicks and clicks of forbidden time known as after hours.

I went to the jukebox around 5:30. I played my songs and went back to finish my session. When Seger came on I thought of myself on an ivory colored Fat Boy with solid steel rims. When that one Beach Boys song came on I wished that they had made more like it. When *Meeting Across The River* played lonely, letting the smooth thick sax through, I thought about the tall lady in K.C. perhaps a bit lonely for some touch.

One From The Ice

After that came *Samba Pa Ti*, and I thought of sentences I would use during my father's eulogy, and that rolled into *Waiting On A Friend* and no thought, just a smooth thick buzz not wanting to see daylight, just the snow against night, and the dense freshness with which it covered everything. But that lasted till just after the song, and then I was drunk, and daylight started to peek through the curtains, and the N started to run more frequently.

I got up, and Paul was still sipping his coffee cup. Everyone was hammered and sloppy, and the guy who would yell at the end of the bar was looking at me, blasted.

"Paul, who's the guy at the end of the bar?" I asked clutching the wood.

"Ahh, oh, that's Hugh. Hugh, say 'ello ta Davey Boy."

"CHEERS FUCKO!" He raised the guy's drink that was asleep on the bar next to him and downed it.

I walked across the street before it got too light out, with hope for the late afternoon. "I know you will," I thought of my father saying as I fought the snow and my pockets for my keys.

FAITH AND SUNDAY

Alberto was holding his daughter's hand as they exited over the marble floors of St. John's into the sun half hidden behind the clouds. The blessed water from the sign of the cross mixed on his forehead with slight beads of sweat that he wiped with a subtle glance of his thumb. His boy holding his mother's hand was shaking Msgr. Torres' hand, and he thought about how beautiful Carol his wife was when he had taken her unexpectedly, passionately in the shower, hoping the kids could not hear just before the eleven thirty mass.

"Caballero! Que pasa, eh?" Monsignor's outstretched hand was extended, warm as old friends' hands tend to be.

"What ya think Monsignor, bring Pettitte back or what?"

"Ah, well you know what I think Alberto. Further he wants to pitch in our lovely new digs. I would hope that money remains the smallest of issues between them."

"Yeah, money's always a small issue with the Yanks."

"I know, I know. Pray for ole 46 though, eh? He's worked hard for us."

One From The Ice

"Yes…he has. I loved your homily today by the way, see you in the week," Alberto said going away, taking his wife in his arm, their kids' steps in front leading the way to the car in back of the church.

"You thought it was a good homily?" Carol asked looking ahead, her breath faintly outlined by early March air.

"I did. I always like the Monsignor's stuff, you know that."

"He kisses your ass because he likes the size of our envelopes."

"Ah…maybe."

"Yeah, maybe my ass. Father Crawford's much better."

"Well, now you're talking about a completely different kind of ass kissing."

"Ah…maybe."

Her hand fell lazily into the back pocket of his Hugo Boss pants. He noticed the new highlights she had been talking about getting and decided that he liked them very much. They enjoyed a good life. She was a good woman, and he found himself still very attracted to her. Her body was still firm save for some dips and changes that life and their kids had brought naturally. Recently, they had been exploring a revitalization between them. Sometimes the fights had gotten so bad that they only spoke to one another in front of the kids, hating the fact that their lives had become typical. But with more time passing, the animosity had started to fade, the storms seemed nearly behind them.

"You felt amazing this morning," he said taking her closer, kissing her flush on her cold cheek that she tilted slightly to give him.

"Let's next weekend…" she paused.

"Let's next weekend what?"

"Let's get rid of our two beautiful children and get a room at the Plaza."

"The Plaza, huh? That little out of the way bed and breakfast?"

"Well?" she smiled almost laughing. "Why not? We can afford it. You can adjust your schedule."

"Yeah we can, and yes, I can."

"And you know my sister and Johnny will take the kids no questions. It's been so long Alberto…it's been too long."

"I don't see why not, baby."

"Good." She sighed. "I'll make the arrangements this week."

"Ah…" Alberto paused, and strangely the sound of Monsignor's voice vibrated in and out of his mind. No words or definitive structure, just tone and pitch. "Let me set it up. I'm pretty sure I can get a suite rated through Zuckerman and his people, so I'll take care of it."

"Okay. I'll call my sister."

Carol's lips had always been one of his favorite features on her. Full always with dark shades of gloss or lipstick, and as they walked, Alberto wanted to kiss her as he had in the shower, his tongue all over them, but quickly he reminded himself of where they were, and settled on just the feeling of pride he had that she was his wife, the pride of how she was raising his children. There were reasons this Sunday, he thought, why he had been noticing everything next to him, and in front of him, words, friends, truth.

"C, honey, would you mind if I caught the …"

"No. I don't mind. I had a feeling you were going to ask. I don't mind, just don't be late please, and don't be hammered. All I have to do is heat it up. I went to Rosario's on Friday."

"Ok."

"Give me the keys, tell your children."

He handed over the familiar sound of his keys and called his children over to him. His daughter Lindsey ran, his son Frankie sauntered perplexed.

"What's the matter champ?"

"Where are YOU going?" he asked sarcastically, looking back at his father the way Alberto looked at his father, the sound of Frankie's sarcasm, his mother Carol's.

"He's going to watch the Knicks game stupid!" Lindsey shouted abruptly waving her arms in any direction they would go.

"OH!!! You don't talk to your brother like that."

"Sorry Daddy."

"Say sorry to your brother Frankie."

"Sorry Frankie," she sighed without care.

"I'll be home for supper kid, couple hours yea?"

"Yeah."

"Yeah?"

"Yeah." Frankie smiled giving and getting kisses from his father who then had him in a bear hug balanced on one knee.

"Think about Tampa this year, and we will talk about it over dinner. Ok Frankie?"

"Really?!" His dark brown eyes fully rose from their sunken position moments ago.

One From The Ice

"Well, yeah. We better get a move on. Spring training's almost over kid. I think we can all use a little trip to Tampa anyways," Alberto said looking at Carol's green eyes, stroking the top of Lindsey's hair.

He stood up and kissed Carol. Carol rubbed her fingers against him just as she used to do when they first started dating and were kissing in public, no one the wiser beneath the surface.

"Don't be late," she whispered. "And bring some dessert…for us I mean, for later."

"Ok." Alberto smiled. He walked several strides and decided to wave, but his family had already started towards their beige Cadillac parked next to the black Cadillac that was the property of St. John's.

The sun was dying in the clouds when Alberto hailed a gypsy cab to the Upper East Side. The traffic was thin, the roads whitened from winter salt. The driver had a hard time slowing for rises of concrete and barely kept to the edge of major potholes now unearthed from the absence of snow, the final fade of winter. The girders of the Queensboro passed out of the corner of his eye with the presence and time of ghosts. The words of Msgr. Torres' homily started to echo in his mind. Carol and his children raw in his memory, fresh in his blood, ran all over his fit body back into his face where the feelings pushed out his eyes in the form of thick tears.

"Give and it shall be given to you. For whatever measure you deal out to others, it will be dealt to you in return."

Alberto swore from the third pew that when Msgr. Torres spoke, his dark eyes highlighted from the gold of his aviator frames, his words were intended directly for him. At that moment, next to his wife and children, every carefully crafted lie and all the happy hour and midnight self-justifications bore themselves inside him as right and wrong.

His father had mistresses, his brother had mistresses, and hopefully Frankie would break the cycle, Alberto thought. He had had one other lover during his twelve-year marriage. Sandy, a secretary for a distributor with which he no longer worked. A gorgeous 24 year-old black woman that understood the relationship would never go anywhere outside the walls of midtown hotels that she put on her Visa, for which in return, Alberto would give her cash and gifts. There was little emotion, which meant easier rationalizations, better constructed lies, and on the advice of Alberto Pauletti Sr. a clean break, no regrets.

It was the previous June when he met Shelley at a high-end fundraiser for Big Brothers Big Sisters of New York City. His company was making a sizable donation and though Alberto was not part of the program himself two of his top executives were, and they had urged him for an appearance.

One From The Ice

Shelley wore a black cocktail dress and black stockings that night. Her little sister Aya was seven and quite in charge of the room with her energy amidst everyone's foregone conclusion that she was indeed special. Aya wore a red satin dress with black shoes, her dark Philippine skin running all the way up into a well-coifed ensemble of curls. It was in fact Aya who noticed Alberto before Shelley. After the photographs of the check, his executives with theirs, Aya appeared, her eyes a little lost and curious.

"She's mine." Shelley appeared relieved as if she had been looking for her. "Seven years old, and she's got it for Italian guys. Oy." She sighed.

"How do you know I'm Italian?"

"Honey, you wear it as well as that suit."

Shelley's hand was well manicured with a faint bit of sweat. After exchanging pleasantries, names, purpose for being there, praise of the program, they moved to backgrounds. Her manners were well practiced, her eyes blue, a touch cloudy. The black cocktail dress was sleeveless and showed her powdered white skin that was marbled with swirls of faint red around her shoulders and the base of her neck. As they talked her self-deprecating wit surprised him. Her body appeared to be more voluptuous than Carol's, though as quick as the comparisons between the two arrived in his mind, they were escorted out just as fast. Her voice was deep but not hoarse or raspy. He could not help but let himself be taken by how she subtly talked with her hands, how her hair was the perfect length for her just below the ear, jet black, stunning, but not in a way to stop a room in its tracks, but rather sexy as the shadows and the private spaces the room held. She called him on every bluff, and no woman had done that in years. He told her that he was married, and all she did was shake her head and say "Oy....let's just play." He could still feel the deep brash feeling in his chest of that night that wove itself over many nights, and many afternoons.

That was last June, now it was March he thought to himself. He felt that he had to end it before the cracks of his secret emotions started to flow, before the guilt seeped into his family and his work, leaving everything he worked for and created a statistic.

"Eighty-sixth and Lexington." Alberto spoke somberly as he wiped his eyes. This would be, had to be the last time he would sneak to her 17th floor apartment. Torres' words still resonated, grated, forced Alberto to deal with a black part of his life that had to be confronted, dealt with, and discarded as soon as time would permit.

"So much of today's practices or ill-practices, what we see, what is reflected, what we settle for, how we have come to give up so easily, is...falls...upon each of us

One From The Ice

evenly. The responsibility is ours. Whether it is in business, in our family, in our word, community, or handshake. Please ask yourselves... 'What am I doing? How am I to blame? Did I try today? Or did I lie today? How can I correct this? How can I help?'

"These are fundamental, common sense questions that we ALL were taught from the earliest of ages, and yet, in our everyday lives, we have lost the sensibility and conviction to answer them and practice what we know is right. Let's today pray for the courage to admit, and right our wrongs, to have an everyday diligence to right, and stay our courses, for something bigger than ourselves, bigger than our selfishness and our short comings."

The cab rolled on Third Avenue. Alberto asked the driver to make a left on 81st Street. On the corner, JoAnne's Wine And Cheese was nearly empty, sparking the warm memory of the summer night when Shelley and he shared their last bottle of Simi red just before he took her for the first time.

On arriving to her building, Alberto noticed first that the doorman was Ted, which put part of himself at ease due to the fact that Ted was the most professional out of the bunch, and no matter how ugly things got, worse to heinous, Ted would be a gentleman and mind his own business. He exited the cab near side, almost forgetting his gloves, ignoring his change.

"Mr. Pauletti a good afternoon to you, sir." Ted rang out in a deep Staten Island accent as he handled a package. "Shall I ring Ms. Cohen for you?"

"Yes Ted, please. How are things with you?"

"Never better, sir." Ted held the building phone lazily to his ear as if it were a part of him.

"How's the clothing business? Fast and furious I bet."

Alberto looked him up and down wondering what he was thinking. 'He knows,' he told himself twice. 'He knows I'm married, what I'm here for. I fuckin' hate doormen.' He found himself creating paranoid scenarios in second long frames before reminding himself that small talk was Ted's craft, and that he ultimately liked him.

"You bet. No rest for designer wholesale."

They smirked politely at each other while Alberto's mind then began to wonder where she could be, and perhaps with whom. He never showed up unexpected, especially on a Sunday. He could hear the faint ring over and over which then blended in with his thoughts of what she might be doing and with whom…over and over. He did not call, text or e-mail. He had no time. He would wait, or come back he told himself. It was worth it, it must be do----

One From The Ice

"Ms. Cohen, hi I have Mr. Pauletti here for you. -----Yes ma'am, you do the same. Go on ahead, Mr. Pauletti. A good day to you."

"Thanks."

There was an elevator waiting which was odd to Alberto. At times, the wait and anticipation had sometimes forced him to take the stairs, causing him to catch his breath along the way, and several minutes in the hallway before knocking on her door. One of those times Shelley caught him while she was waiting and wondering what was taking so long. They laughed about it all that afternoon and Alberto could sense that she cared for him very much, possibly more than she would ever, could ever allow herself to admit. The hum of the elevator carried the weight of Alberto's sighs, putting him at peace for several moments between the Ninth and Fifteenth floors.

"I know it's Sunday." He spoke awkwardly meeting her at her door.

"Yeah, it's Sunday."

"Are you alone?"

"Don't be an ass. Come in."

She went to take his coat as she always had, but he waved her off. "What's wrong?" she asked standing in front of him.

Alberto walked past her two steps to the kitchen island that separated the living room, where they had had sex many times, where they conversed over whatever she had in the refrigerator, sometimes in the late hours, sometimes both of them on the run after a quick afternoon meeting. He thought about her habit of leaning against it, bracing herself while they kissed goodbye. Then his mind went blank as if he were ten again being asked by his parents why he was stealing his father's Parliaments. He glanced at her face and for the first time during their relationship saw a truly worried look on it. It was sincere, intense, and fell warm inside him.

"You're scaring me," she said definitively.

In the living room the computer was on and open to a spread sheet letting him know that she had been working, explaining why she had been late to the phone. The fabric on her sofa was grey and expensive. There were no lights on, Alberto looked through the sliding doors past her balcony, and the sun had completely gone, leaving the remaining white ash color of the day just before dark. In those instances, there became no Monsignor. No Carol. No Lindsey. No Frankie.

"I had to see you."

"Here I am."

One From The Ice

She was wearing a grey Tom Petty concert tee that formed to her body from many years of wear. It faintly outlined the sides of her breasts which still very much aroused him. Her blue shorts ran baggy below her knees with a yellow trim donning a University of Michigan insignia, questions of her wearing panties further gave way to her body, and her giving it to him with no questions, no limitations.

"Are you ok? I've never seen you like this."

Her voice reminded him of how safe and alive he felt with her in her apartment. No responsibilities except to please her, to make the most out of their time and sex, their conversations, thoughts and laughter. All the guilt had become frozen somewhere outside of him without any coercion or force, all Alberto felt was right. Right in his being there, right in his thoughts, damn the rest.

"I came here to have you."

"So have me."

Shelley pulled her shirt overhead and took down her shorts, stepping out of them one leg at a time. She waited for him, not wearing panties or a bra, giving Alberto plain day sight of her. He felt her entire body over before kissing her, handling every inch of what she offered, of what he could not turn down. The quiet of the room was painted by their familiar sounds, his clothes being taken off, her tongue in and out of his mouth, the pressure of their want being exhausted through gasps.

"You came over here to break it off didn't you?" she asked in between kisses on his neck and his shoulders. He kept pulling at her blindly, burying himself in her skin, and in her breaths.

SAUTÉED ON THE SHORE

It was hot, and as I recall, we were getting killed that night. I was working sauté and fry. Rick was next to me in the trenches on broiler, calling ticket times and orders. We split salads and desserts whichever one of us had time. Rick was on fire. Still one of the single greatest performances I have witnessed. As calm as any sweating man over a broiler could be. I was clammy and nervous, but in such a zone I did not have time to think about it, just to deal with it.

"Catherine sweetheart, tell Bianca we could use a couple more back here please." Rick yelled out and it took some time for Catherine to answer, which meant, she was in the weeds as well, and there was no sign of business letting up.

"I know you're busy too honey, but were both dying back here." I saw him glance over his shoulder.

"Okay. A minute though alright, guys?"

"That's fine, dear. Thank you."

"Owen? What do you say?" she asked in her smarmy Tom's River voice.

"Thank you, Catherine." She obviously was still not pleased with me for not calling her back after we had sex last week. But that would have to wait. I was hot, and I knew that my soda was going to be a little different from Rick's, which made me even more agitated.

"Jeeves, how's that re-cook for the Camaro?" The re-cook was a pasta primavera and almost done, the Camaro was Joe Rini, the owner's son. He was a pretentious want to be actor who spent summers at the restaurant, and the rest of the time pretending in the city, all the time whacked on coke. His primavera died, due to the fact he didn't modify it with "no tomatoes" and the other common knowledge bit that he could barely handle a doorknob, let alone a three-table station. Of course, it was my fault. "Sixty seconds." I was right on.

"I don't want to hear it from the ole man."

"Neither do I. Thirty seconds."

On top of that I was working two chicken pestos over angel hair, breading coconut shrimp, continually dropping fries, a chicken scaloppini with no artichokes, and soon the ole man would be back for his chicken caesar. (It used to be filet, or chops until a recent visit to his doctor. At least that was the gossip going around.) In the meantime, I could not wash the pans as quickly or as well as I needed with the orders coming in

One From The Ice

that fast. Ortiz the dishwasher fell asleep on the beach last night and wouldn't be out of jail until another hour. We were damn busy.

"Owen?"

"Fifteen seconds."

The printer kept vibrating and getting on my nerves. "I need some more apple chutney, and you got another pesto adding on marsala. I got the pasta." Without him saying that, I would have been done, the ole man would have been back there, and Rick knew it.

"Thanks."

He was like a metronome back and forth. Never lost it, never threw anything, never saw him make a quick move, never saw him get agitated, for as much as he drank, never saw him drunk. All Rick did was quietly crank out covers, chuckle a few times, and drink. And, under the vacuum of the hoods, the sporadic twists of flames, my grunting, the slamming of plates, he just kept even. Even in the heat.

BANG!!! The tested wood of the "in" door slammed against the tile of the wall. I didn't even look up; I knew exactly who it was.

"Let's have it."

"Fifteen seconds Joe, don't go anywhere."

"Where the fuck am I gonna go? Plate my fucking pasta."

"Take it easy Joe, we're all really…"

"Yeah, I know Rick. Fuck easy. Hey, tough guy, plate my fucking dish."

I concentrated on the green and yellow of the zucchini, and how much oil, light, and how it spread evenly over everything, tossing it twice, lowering its heat.

"Look Gallagher, I'm not gonna fuckin' beg, I'm gonna come back there, hit you once, plate it, and that's it."

"Joe, I don't want it coming back, ten seconds, c'mon man." My voice wavered, but I decided not to give it up just then, meanwhile I concentrated on everything else.

"Rick, was the matter wit' yer boy?"

"Plate it Owen," Rick said calmly.

I looked over, Rick nodded to do it intently, then he turned a filet and two chops. I lowered the heat under the primavera more, almost off. I looked above the sink to see an empty spot where the pasta bowls should have been. I sighed deep, and started to round the line for more.

"What the fuck?! What's this?"

One From The Ice

I walked with my head down just past his legs to the right of him. I bent down, picked up two armfuls of pasta bowls, and stood to see the Camaro facing me, smiling as if he knew many things that I did not.

"Why didn't you just fuckin' ask me for one? C'MON!" He exclaimed dipping and swiveling his head, arms outstretched.

"Here you go, Rick." Catherine came in with the drinks. I glanced back stepping aside the Camaro who dipped his shoulder into the bowls knocking about five of them to the floor. I remember setting the rest of the stack in the window facing him.

"Feelin' strong, fucko?" he asked tightening his shoulders.

"Owen! Plate the dish!" I heard Rick's voice raise but didn't realize the importance of it. It was the first time I had ever squared off and really looked at the Camaro. He seemed smaller. I remember him trying to be smug.

"What're ya' gona do? Get my fuckin' food! YOU KNOW WHO THE FUCK I AM?! YOU KNOW WHO THE FUCK I AM?! " I tried to step around him again, but he put out his shoulder sharp into my chest, sneaky, so Rick and Catherine could not see. And that's when I went.

I rose right in front of him, throwing my right, twisting my fist just like my ole man when he would hit the heavy bag in the basement. His face was not hard or brittle like some of the others I had hit in the past. Everything about it was clean, and I remember him trying to rise up too late. I must have caught the whole barrel because he lost his legs, and fell back into the black trash bags around the dish pit. I looked down into his brown eyes, *ladies' eyes* I thought, his mother's maybe, and he looked at me with nothing and blood, running either from his nose or mouth I couldn't tell. I couldn't hear anything but the vacuum of the hoods. Turning scared, I picked up one of the bowls and went back to work.

BANG!!! The tested wood of the "in" door smacked against the white tile of the wall. I raised the heat under the primavera and flipped it twice, too scared to look up. I just kept working. I felt Rick glancing at me, then his grill, back and forth.

"This MOTHER FUCKER!!!" I heard the Camaro start to yell.

"Calm down!" The ole man probably heard the bowls from the bar. I heard him yell, then feet crunching through the shards of beige porcelain, then the muffled grunts of Rini restraining his son. I tossed the primavera, dropped the coco shrimp, and rinsed out a pan for the marsala, not looking back.

One From The Ice

"This fuckin' cocksucker's dead! You fucking cunt motherfucker! I swear to CHRIST!!! You're a fuckin' dead man. Fuckin' dead!!!"

"Joseph! Calm…"

"Fuck that!! Are you…"

"JOSEPH!!! Calm the fuck down, go and get cleaned up." Things went silent again, and I felt I might be in real trouble that I would not be able to get out of. I threw the marsala wine in the pan, oil, a bit of butter, the mushrooms, and then went to lightly bread the breasts. I heard the weathered wood of the "out" door bounce off the Kelley green plaster of the dining room wall.

"Gallagher?"

"Yes sir." I breaded the two breasts and placed them in the pan over low heat.

I tried to imagine that nothing was happening, that if I kept working, nothing would happen, so I pulled the shrimp up, shook the fry basket, and tried desperately to keep my shoulders square to the stove.

"Gallagher?"

"Yes sir."

"Turn the fuck around." And so I did. His face squinted tan with all the resiliency of hard living and experience. I fixed on the gold of his pinky ring halfway in the window. One time shortly after I had started and Rick and I were smoking out back he told me not to let the ole man's subtleness fool me, that his silk-like silent movements were to be taken seriously, that Rini used to hold seminars in fine dining in Chicago with the hotel unions, and in San Francisco when the micro-breweries started to go nation wide. He catered a Super Bowl once, (which one is always a great debate that Rini never divulges) had the guts to openly piss on the coffee craze in *Cranes*, and then again in *Wine Spectator*. "Well connected. A very nice, well connected, fair man." That's all anybody ever said, so I respected it as that. I had just hit his son, we were in the middle of a rush, and he was staring me down in his kitchen.

"Is it ready?"

"Yes."

"Plate it." He turned from the line kicking the shards into a pile. As I turned I saw Catherine go for a broom. I raised the heat and tossed it three more times, then raised the heat on the marsala, my hands shaking, cold. When I slid it into the bowl, I noticed that the pasta was a little overdone around the edges. I used the parsley to cover it up, but I felt confident when I handed it over to the ole man. His tiny hand grabbed it and then stopped. That's when I heard the printer start to go off again, but Rick remained silent.

"We'll discuss this as soon as business eases up."

"Yes sir."

"This better be the best fucking primavera he's ever had, no?"

"Yes sir."

"You're very lucky I know the score in my house."

"Yes sir."

"Get back to your covers."

"Yes sir." I turned and tried to put all the wonderment of what was to come out of my mind. I dove into the stove and everything that I had working on it.

"Catherine, check on Joey's tables. I know you're busy honey, but they need attention."

"Yes sir."

"Rick."

"Yes boss?"

"Throw a tuna filet on there in about twenty minutes. I'm gonna have a nicoise salad tonight."

"Twenty minutes?"

"Dinner's gonna be a little late tonight." I heard the weathered flesh of his hand push the "out" door open.

"Owen, start two shrimp alfredos, a side of coco shrimp, and sell me those chicken pestos. You put me in the weeds, kid."

"I've never seen you in the weeds," I said not looking up as I started the orders.

"Yeah. Just don't sit me in the trash, huh?"

"Fuck you." I saw him smile out of the corner of my eye, then turn for the printer.

"That's three shrimp alfredos all day…Hagler."

"Fuck you."

I was supposed to meet up with my friend Phil and take it to the shore. I decided I was going to do that with or without a job. I needed it. I needed a beer. I put everything else out of my mind, and concentrated on the orders, the shore, and beer. The tickets didn't stop. Rick and I just kept plating them.

One From The Ice

THE PORCH

I always mark the fresh seasons with symbols that have lasted me for some time. Winter and jazz, autumn and Neil Young, summer becoming whatever starts or finishes a healthy sweat exasperating under hazy or clear nights.

Spring however, hints at everything with possibility that makes my stale St. Paddy's day liver clean, a session of catch a reality, a coat of vibrancy on things lethargic that lets the provocative out of my filthy winter ridden apartment.

I stepped into this particular spring on a Thursday after an ordinary shift at the "Rock." Walking down Sixth Avenue is always a pain in the ass that time of day, but makes those first couple bottles of Bud that much more rewarding and leads to whatever dinner is to be that night. It was a fine time to get a stool at Fiddler's too, right before the happy hour puke gobbled everything with their young bullshit. I cannot complain, more often than not I end up with one of their ladies.

A week before day light savings, no leaves on the trees yet, but the air has definitely changed and thawed out the pavement, the buildings and the gyro carts. Baseball has just started (thank Christ) and I can't wait to feel sore after the season's first catch with my brother. I had guessed the bark of the trees were still damp in Central Park. In thinking of all of it as a whole, I was reminded of the three-stepped raised concrete porch with a fresh white painted fence that wrapped around. It belonged to Irving and Mamie Soderquist who had lived across the street from me while I was growing up.

"Now, watcha gotta do is, make sure the plastic wrap is really tight around the bowl so, when the ole man sits down he can't see it. So he starts to shit right?"

"Irving!!!"

"He'll be yelling so loud, oh man, I'd love to hear that."

"Irving Soderquist!"

I was eight or nine when I started hanging out on the Soderquists' porch. Mr. Soderquist worked for the city in Central Park on the trees. He was thin in the face, and muscles bulged in his forearms that were attached to thick birched hands. He slumped in his chair almost hiding in it like a sniper, and when he walked, he glided slightly hunched. He never combed what was left of his grey strands, and sometimes he would shave, and sometimes he would have a beard, but most of the time it was scruff. I remember he was always tanned, and I could never tell what color his eyes were. My mother said they were a crazy gray, yet I always found sincerity in their beady, insane, mouse like movements.

One From The Ice

"Behave." Mamie Soderquist would say as she laughed and got up from beside him to finish work she had started hours earlier. Mamie, a little light headed naturally though wise from what Irving, her children, and the years had put her through, retained much of her attractiveness and traces of her youth in her laugh, large brown eyes and skin complexion. I remember seeing pictures of her in her early twenties when Pete was two and Danny Boy had just been born. She honestly could have been a model, but instead she fell in love and had kids with Irving. One of the most generous ladies I have ever known, and she would tease and flirt with me about girls.

"See that cherry blossom there?" Irving pointed a stained finger to a white-blossomed tree as he smacked a tin of Copenhagen with the other.

"I stuck that in for Mamie in '75."

He took the stained finger, opened the shiny lid and pinched thick dark mulch fastening it into a prepared space between his lower lip and gum.

"I had to get special permission and all that other horses' ass shit. It's even registered in her name. Helps when you know people. Remember that."

He looked at me sharply and padded the dip deeper with his tongue, then spat casually over the white of the railing.

"Wanna pinch?"

He leaned in and extended the tin in my direction. I wanted a pinch. I wanted to spit and pad it down with my tongue. I could smell its distinctly fresh evergreen scent, and I wanted to dive in to feel the brown of its dirty color. I leaned in cautiously.

"Goddamitt! Irving Soderquist!"

I tore back into my chair as Mamie holy yelled through the door. Irving remained still, and he smiled as he presented the dip to me and motioned for me to come get it.

"What? He's a man. I'm being polite."

"He's eight you filthy bastard! Put the snuff away."

He retreated as casually as he had started, and he leaned back and put the tin into his shirt pocket, spitting another full solid bomb clear over the railing.

"Do you want the broth over the gravy?"

"Mix 'em both, you know, over the potatoes and the vegetables like I like."

One From The Ice

"Over everything?"

"Yeah. Christ. Over everything."

"Well? How the hell should I know?"

"How'd the zucchinis come out?"

"Oh Irving, just wait till you see them."

"Good."

He nodded his head and put his foot on the patio table and simultaneously scratched his crotch. Mamie gave a once through my hair and went back inside. It was where I first differentiated smells and sounds of spring, anticipation of summer and its nights. Where I was allowed to pick my nose and cuss because Irving did. I remember just him and I sitting there alone watching the street, begging every second for him to say or do something. He'd cough heavily, pound his chest, scratch the side of his face, and spit over the railing, all in uniformed, symphonic, movements.

As dusk approached, the traffic got thicker and carried a lazy energy, mostly content. The wind sometimes would whip a wind of winter at the end of its gusts, and I remember always wishing to be warmer, then quickly putting it out of my mind as I glanced back at Irving with his marred green uniform opened to his naval, his pants unbuckled and half zipped, showing the band of his boxers. Sometimes he would walk around like that in boots in the winter.

"Remember Dickey Sterkel?"

How could I forget the fat bastard with a worse mouth than Irving in the gold Dodge pickup that had a plow on the front year round?

"Yes."

"Back before, shit, way back, this was back when him and I used to drink. Way back."

The white aluminum door opened and latched, Mamie thumbed her hand down my cheek and curled up into Irving as she shook off a chill and smiled.

"Remember Dickey Sterkel?"

"Oh, Christ."

She rolled into a laugh and covered her mouth while Irving grinned and cascaded the mustard tint of his teeth, cocked his head, and launched a brown bomb clear of Mamie and the railing.

"Please don't, Irving." She begged playfully.

"One night…December…'77."

"Seventy-Eight."

One From The Ice

"You sure, baby?"

"Oh, how the hell would you remember, you were wrecked the whole time."

"Seventy-Eight. Anyway, I sent him home after cards from up the…what the fuck?"

Mamie rolled her eyes, broke her smile and turned to me pausing. She cleared her throat with her hand over her chest, and then broke back into her smile.

"Dickey Sterkel, Irving, Tommy McManus, and Roy James, or…"

"Nah." He padded down the dip deeper into the left side of his mouth, and then pinched it into shape while he thought.

"Andrew Frank." They said in unison.

"That's right." Mamie broke. "I always confused them because they both had two first names."

"Frank owned the bar, c'mon."

"That's right, The Shrub Club. They named it that Davey because they used fertilizer that Irving took home from the park for the urinals."

"Yeah, and ice, you know, for the pissers."

"Anyways, Andrew always kept the boys later on Friday to play cards seeing as they didn't have to work on Saturdays, you know."

"Unless we had overtime."

"Right. Anyways."

"Drew used to lock us in, you know, after closing. He had this space in the back he used for parties and such, Fridays around eleven he'd give us the thumbs up or down."

"Usually up." Mamie stiffened, biting her lip.

"Anyways, the three of us would stumble around setting up cause, by this point, shots, beers, for four hours, we were pissed."

"That means drunk, Davey."

"Ok."

"So we'd set up the table and chips, Drew would finish his shit, and we'd play cards till, you know, daylight or, whatever."

"Yeah, well, it's a wonder you…"

"Well, that's what happens when you know cops right? You get away with shit like that."

Irving opened his mouth, coughed violently for a few moments, hacking, pushing forward, and collecting the phlegm with the dip juice,

One From The Ice

launching it almost to the sidewalk. His arm remained around Mamie never disturbing her position. She curled into him sometimes, padding his chest. Most of the time she looked silently into the street.

"Anyways, one night, fucking Sterkel…"

"Watch your f-bombs, Irving."

"Sterkel gets out of his head. It wasn't just booze either, his brother in law scored half…"

"It wasn't just booze!!!" Mamie interjected.

"Anyways, he almost tosses the joint, and Drew's had enough. I mean Drew let us stay because most of the time he'd take our money. But once Dickey started pissing in corners and throwing things at all the bottles because he hated his ex-wife, we roughed him up a little and sent him home."

"You beat him up?" I dared to ask. There was a pause and Mamie cocked her head to Irving's chin.

"Ga head, tell him."

"Dickey started throwing punches, the jukebox, dartboards, the taps, just throwing fists. So, we had to calm him down."

"And how'd you do that tough guy?" Mamie asked sarcasticly.

"We set up like a triangle around him." Irving configured a triangle with his hands and looked at the space in between smiling dryly.

"Drew stepped up and hit him in the stomach. He was pissed. I just gave him a little Charlie horse to get him stable, you know, stop him from running everywhere. McManus cleaned his jaw 'cause he was pissed at him for some money Dickey owed him, but more because he fucked the game. McManus loved those Friday nights. Thought he had a chance every time."

"Irving, your language. C'mon! He's eight, and I don't want to hear it from his mother. Watch your fucking f-bombs!!!" She realized what she said, and laughed.

"So after all of it…Drew decides to buy McManus and I breakfast at the Andropolis. It was a diner where the fuckin' Pep Boys is now. Your old man would remember."

"It was funny Davey, Irving would be there for breakfast, and sometimes we'd go there for dinner and have the same waiter." Mamie proclaimed in a girlish tone.

"We sober up, the sun's up, Drew catches a cab, I walked McManus to his car. I rounded just the corner right over there." He pointed his stained finger at the corner I had rounded a million times,

One From The Ice

where things "happened" for everybody in the neighborhood, and suddenly the corner took on deeper meaning.

"Swear to Christ, three feet of snow, I round the corner, stumbling, I get my balance and hear sirens, look up, Sterkel's running at me, ass naked, his cock back and forth, his wife Sheila and the fire department right behind him."

"His lip was like a fucking balloon!" Mamie broke laughing.

"He ran past me holding his thigh screaming, 'Help is on the way Irving! Help is on the way!' His wife, fire trucks screaming past."

It was the hardest I had ever laughed to that point. Mamie and Irving smiled and laughed with me, and I did not feel eight years old, and I was glad that none of the other kids on the block were there with us.

Mamie wiped her eyes, and Irving took the wet mulch from his mouth and flung it into the bushes to the left of the porch. He coughed twice, hacked up more phlegm, and launched it onto the sidewalk beyond the short lawn. The three of us sat in silence for sometime, then I would break out into laughter thinking of Dickey, and that made Irving smile and Mamie laugh and point affectionately.

"Davey, honey how many girlfriends do you have?"

"Yeah, have you gotten laid yet?"

"Shut up, Irving."

"You find the drawer with all the nudies and goodies in it?"

"Shut up!"

She slapped him across the chest as she got up quickly and scared me as she slammed the door behind her. I looked at Irving who was looking at me smiling, gesturing for an answer. I didn't know what he meant at the time, so I just kept silent.

"Nah, Dickey's a good a man though. Not many like him." I knew what a good man was because everyone told me that my father was, but I never imagined him drunk or naked running up the street.

"They need more cherry trees in the city out here. They're indigenous to California. Pretty wood. Goddamn pretty wood. You ever see cherry furniture like a chest or dresser or any shit like that?"

"No." I shook my head.

"Fuck California, though. Fuckin' people live in bubbles."

I watched him move with authority and grace seemingly not moving at all. For as dirty as he was, or how people judged him, his image, his mannerisms and confidence shaped and stuck, just like spring.

"Cherry's definitely my favorite. I wish New York had more cherry wood."

One From The Ice

"You don't drink anymore?"

"Nah. Shit'll kill you."

"My mom says chewing tobacco will kill you, too."

"Yeah, a lot slower though, least in my case." He licked his lips and coughed.

"You play baseball yet?" He turned to me; I shook my head disgusted with myself for not trying out yet.

"Start!" he said facing back to the street. "It takes care of a lot of things. Even if you suck, play."

Cars' tires sounded crisper, horns a little more abundant, a little more of women shown, school was almost finished, my head got slapped a bit more. It was before I discovered Yankee Stadium and music, right when I discovered breasts and the women who had them.

"You know what you should do? One night, late, shit in a paper bag, sneak out, put it right in front of O'Brien's door, set it on fire, bang on the door, run like hell."

The door opened and Irving sat up. Mamie was holding a plate full of food that smelled similar to my mother's. She set it on the table in front of him then handed him a rolled up paper towel containing a knife and a fork. She sat next to him and handed him a thick blue glass with lots of ice that he drank immediately. He gouged forkfuls of dripping beef and mashed potatoes, and the muscles in his head flexed with intensity, and I sat silently, watching them both.

Just as always when I felt another story brewing and my closeness to them was drawing even nearer mom would yell for supper, and the grown ups would wave to each other.

"Davey honey, safe home, careful on the street, sweetie." Mamie would wave.

"Yeah, make sure the wrap's good and tight around the bowl."

As I think of it now, all the laundry between them was washed, all their secrets forgiven, and kept between them. Though I was too young to realize it then, those afternoons held security that most people never achieve, confidence I fight for, survival, and the porch that enters my mind every first spring, right before dinner.

One From The Ice

THE QUIET MORNING

She heard him stirring, tiny noises just beyond the crack of his door. She moved gently so as not to disturb her husband next to her. His sleep was more important given his new job, his career. Her nightgown ran just below her knees and was made from thin, chintzy fabric. At this point, she was grateful just to have something to wear at night. They were not quite on their feet. She kept moving as silently as their two-bedroom rental would allow. She had grown accustomed to the cracks at different spots on the floor. The one, a stride out of the bathroom, and a near inch dip to the right of the kitchen sink. Nearly the entire surface of the living room was under the green area rug they had gotten as a wedding present from her sister and brother in law. What they had gotten from his mother she had bought from Sears using her employee discount.

Her husband was a sound sleeper that she adored, able to watch his stoic chin resting, her arms around his strong build. *It was her time to watch and protect* she would think to herself every morning just before she rose. Late October brought her birthday and their one-year anniversary, freshness as always, fuller this year, their first October with their first-born…a son.

Her fear of the unknown, a young mother whose insides were full with child, was gone. He was healthy and progressing, and she was healthy (though she did not care so much for her own health). Future fears would come soon enough and every morning with many more to come. These were her initial thoughts.

She filled the orange kettle and placed it over the blue gas flames as they ignited in the shape of a crown on the back right burner of the stove. Her favorite mug was one she had bought in college with a print of the Norman Rockwell painting *Looking Out at Sea*. It was her favorite because she had never been to a place like the one depicted in the painting, and she wished that the very old man who resembled her father would be there when she finally made it. It was the only mug she never broke. She put two spoonfuls of Folger's in the mug leaving the spoon inside prepared, and turned to put her husband's jacket on, long and thick, then her sneakers worn from the summer, dingy, that she used like slippers.

Outside the driveway was gravel, and every time she stepped diligently so as not to twist her ankle, she always did. It was fifty feet down to the edge of the two-lane road where the paper was flung at the foot of the mailbox. Still dark, she breathed with exaggerated breaths to catch shadows of her exhales in rhythm with the sound her feet made

One From The Ice

over the gravel, down, and back up, eyes watering with the slight brisk wind of her mouth.

Once back inside she would listen immediately for her boy and almost always, within thirty seconds would hear him toss, perhaps yelp or simply wail if he was feeling that way. The kettle was heating almost to the whistle, hot enough for the coffee, she mixed, stirred, and returned it to its burner, reduced the heat, and saved it warm for her husband. The first tiny sips burned but she took them anyway, quickening her blood, more alert than she was before. It was the time when things were new before routine would settle in her bones, her routines that she would pass on to more children who would take up the peak years of her life, but for now everything was electric and rich.

More sips went down easier each time, three or four times until the mug was half full, and by the time she would return, it would be cold, and she would be ready for a second cup. The water that remained in the pot would be for her husband.

The baby's food was always to be prepared first. Sometimes if she was not feeling well her husband would do it the night before, but those times were few and far between and usually flawed. Sometimes she would have to bring her boy out from the crib early to stop him from crying, and when he was secure in his high chair his eyes would move around following her, and sometimes he would smile. This was because of his gas the doctor had told her, but something inside her said different so she chose to believe that instead.

The baby's favorites were pears and apples, generally anything sweet. He gagged on the vegetables unless they were fresh carrots mashed, not from a jar. In a medium saucepan set aside from the others, she filled his bottle up halfway with water and usually glanced over the headlines of international news that interested her. His bib was one of six, this particular morning, a Cleveland Indians bib, a gift from his uncle, her brother who had played five years in their minor league system as a catcher and had been brought up for fourteen days with the big club before retiring to teach.

She pulled his high chair from the corner. His "feeding space" was in the center of the kitchen in view from the kitchen table, the living room, and the hallway to the bedrooms and the bathroom. His dish was plastic and blue with a Walt Disney depiction of Pooh and Eeyore. His spoon was covered at the end by pink rubber, and he had started to bite down on it leaving small marks. Sometimes during his afternoon naps as she washed his dishes she would run her fingers along the tiny marks and cry.

One From The Ice

Once the Gerber's was placed properly in his dish she set it aside at the edge of the counter and started in on her husband's breakfast and lunch. It did not take very long for breakfast; they only sat down together for it on Sundays. Usually it was whatever fruit was in season, his coffee light and sweet, maybe if he woke early enough five minutes of toast with butter and/or tea with milk. Habits he had picked up from his parents, his mother from County Cork, his dad from Wexford.

Lunch was always brown paper bagged found in bulk in the large bottom drawer to the right of the sink. Five days a week it consisted of fruit and a deli meat sandwich with no mayo. Sometimes there would be leftovers from the night before, and she would sternly remind him to bring home the empty Tupperware containers. The genesis of a major fight had been a lasagna container he did not bring home for a week. She shouted and he laughed, then she laughed, and the next day it was home and cleaned. On some occasions if there was any extra money for a Thursday or Friday, maybe the last day before a holiday he would buy lunch.

At or near this time she would sweep the paper once more and call for her boys to get up. This would serve two purposes; the first and obvious objective to awaken her husband, the other to let the baby know it was time, and that she was on her way.

Her husband stirred, never grumpy genuinely tired. She never minded his morning breath and always caught him on his way to the bathroom for a kiss and a hug.

"Hello, my baby." The light flickered and burst into the crib. Her eyes were wide as they searched out any mishaps, anything unusual that could have occurred during the night.

"How's my boy, huh? OH! Somebody needs to be changed, right away! Yes Sir! You stink, Boyo!"

The changer was a gift from his parents, the only brand new top of the line item they owned. It was from a small chain of appliance stores from which her father-in-law had retired. It had three drawers where she kept morning clothes and day clothes mixed, socks and night ware in the middle, and at the bottom were tubes of Vaseline, A&D Ointment, powder, and miscellaneous small toys she gave him if he were crying, restless while she needed him to be still.

The inspective mindset continued once he was cleaned up. Sometimes he would get a small rash. The first time she noticed an irritation she yelled as if the child had turned blue which caused her husband to act immediately as the Marines had taught him, pushing her out of the way, looking, turning to her as he said firmly "watch him" and left for a moment and returned with something she could not see. His

One From The Ice

back was turned to her, she waited in a frantic gaze, his arms flailed and worked on his firstborn for what seemed like hours. She held her breath dying, then he turned and calmly handed his son over brandishing a clean diaper. "His first diaper rash, Hun." Her defiant silence had lasted 45 minutes.

"Come on baby, let's feed you."

He was happy. His head bobbed gently against her cheek. Just passing the bathroom, he jerked his neck and slammed the top of his forehead into her cheekbone. It hurt her more than him, and he giggled again. He squirmed in his chair and pounded his tiny fists. She put the bib on settling him gradually. She turned the burner on to warm the bottle and sat to feed him.

"Hey babe…is my red long sleeve in the wash?"

"The one from my mother, or the one from Taylor?"

"Taylor."

"Yes. But the one from my mother should be hanging in there."

"No, it's too special that one from your mother."

"Your daddy's so mean to Grandma, don't you listen to him little boy."

"He won't have to, in time he'll figure it out on his own."

His voice came crawling in and his son responded immediately as he looked into his father's direction wide eyed, mouth open.

"See look, he knows already. Don't ya, kiddo? See?"

"You're a jerk."

She tilted her head for a kiss. He kissed her, then his boy on the head.

"Coffee on?"

"Yes, and I made you that ham and turkey sandwich for lunch that you wanted."

"Ah, good."

"Can you stay a minute here with us?"

"I can't baby. I got a conference before first bell. I'll be home early, though."

"Oh, good."

He put his coat and penny loafers on, his tie undone around his neck. He took his brown bag of lunch, a red delicious apple, his briefcase waiting by the door, three sips of coffee.

"Your mother coming today?"

One From The Ice

"Yes. Sister too."

"Well…all my love."

"I hate you."

"I know. But it's a damn good hate."

"Don't curse in front of our son."

A smile and two more kisses and it became like many more mornings to come, just the two of them. After the bottle and more glances through the paper, the sun was lighting the living room through the big picture window looking out onto the two-lane road then to the empty hills that were blue until the day shone their colors. She tried not to miss the sun's full ascent in the rocker with him, before she would put him on the rug to play on his own. His back as she took him from the chair was always relaxed. He felt warm, now content not to move against her, his breath in and out such as a purring cat. She smoothed over the indentations on his head, which the doctor said were normal. His hair was black, but the doctor said that it would probably change. In bursts on the walk over, he would recognize light and maybe routine such as his father's voice, he would lift his head forward and sideways, and she could feel a little of his saliva running down her neck that she damped with a cloth.

She began to rock back and forth, back and forth in their black stained garage sale rocker that was an unsightly piece of joke-ridden furniture; however, it was the most used piece in the apartment. He would make noises that would intertwine with the muffled creaking of the floorboards. There was no other feel like his skin against hers, no smell to match it. Her girlhood dreams had been exceeded, her love and all of its angles realized, taking on prisms of responsibility making life real, purposeful, and just as so many more mornings to come, the sun rose over the hills, the two lane road, the mailbox, to give everything color, to leave just the two of them…back and forth.

One From The Ice

THE TANK

It was a late Saturday afternoon in a particularly cool July. I felt guilty about not being able to make the scene at my friend Huey Lay's show. I told him to meet me at the corner of 50th and Eighth Avenue and that I had a surprise for him. We had been drinking Harvey Wallbangers since February so I met him with a bottle of Galliano. He smiled slow and between the horns and a siren slowly cooed "Aaaahhh yeah." He then told me to stand out in front of another liquor store, then to an alley between the Seventh Avenue subway station and a K.F.C. I had an idea of what was going on so I dipped around the corner to the Belly Deli for some oj and two empty coffee cups. With a pint of Smirnoff and the rest of our fixings Huey got good and ready for his show, and I got ready for my shift in the coalmines of the food service industry.

"I can't believe you didn't get off tonight," Huey said sipping, then putting the bottles in his bag next to his guitar case.

"I know. I had a feeling I would not be able to."

"I guess." He smiled his Huey smile poignantly and rubbed my shoulder.

I was really pissed as the alcohol started to hit my system with a nice thick, warm wave. I tried to think about who might be able to cover for me last minute. But the checklist came up empty. The "Fine Wine" shows had become an event at the coalmines of the food service industry, so anyone capable had already taken off for the night's festivities.

"You know, I could probably give up my Saturday shift," I said, half sip in my mouth.

"Do it. Let's get some Chimay at the Castle before."

"Not tonight. I mean…from tonight on, for good."

"You should do it."

"WE should do it. Regardless if you have a show."

"That's fuckin' dangerous."

"We're drinkin' Wallbangers in an alley off 50th."

"Let's do it."

After that, I gave up my Saturday night to the coked out lesbian who welcomed the extra scratch to cover and probably further her habits. It had been a striking move to everyone including my peculiar general manager, which caused me to wonder just how long I could get away with it. For the time being, it was worth the shot.

One From The Ice

The first Saturday Huey and I had dinner at a French café in the East Village. The steak au poivre was his favorite so we had two. It was a little over done and nothing compared to the quality of the crème brule or the escargot in garlic butter with warm baguette. Close to the end of the second bottle of bordeaux, Huey and I could not laugh anymore for fear of shitting ourselves, so we sat resting, letting in the sounds of Avenue A, metal against porcelain, mixing with smooth euro acid jazz and inaudible conversations.

"Man, it feels good to be off on a Saturday," I said sucking my teeth, reaching for my wine.

"I know. I wish Jerry could be here. He's stuck in that shit hole tonight."

"Maybe he should start requesting Saturday nights off after this week as well," I laughed.

"Maybe he could," Huey said serious.

"You know, that's not such a far stretch, I mean if we all bang out shifts during the week, Saturdays should be ripe to take off."

"Ah man, that'd be great."

"Bigger than great. That's just limitless fuckin' debauchery running naked in the streets."

Huey laughed in his way when he was laughing hard. Holding it in at first, and then letting it out in cool easy intervals, his eyes filled with sincerity.

We finished the night in a blur talking about rock-n-roll past and gone. At the moment Huey was listening to Shirley Bassey and Radiohead's cover of Carly Simon's *Nobody Does It Better* which he said was the sexiest song he had heard in the past two years. I was trying to turn him onto Dove's *Last Broadcast*, and Groove Armada, the latter of which was turned onto me by my friend Denver who many, many women thought was the sexiest thing in Manhattan.

The next day at the start of our Sunday shift, still drunk a bit, we pulled Jerry Maxx aside and told him of our plans. He ran his fingers through his thick black shrub he called hair in a brilliant perplexed state, a sort of cross between Mel Gibson in *Lethal Weapon* part one and Chris Lloyd's Reverend Jim. His thick brown eyes could not contain his madness. We knew just then that we were onto something special, potentially harmful to our well being, seductive as hell.

During that next week of work I somehow got Jerry Maxx to work the same shifts as Huey and I and scheduled the same for the following week with both Saturdays in the free and clear. "The Fine Wines" did not have another show for a month, so all the three of us had

One From The Ice

to do was "keep our noses clean and our uniforms dirty" as I had liked to tell them. Huey and Jerry Maxx had no idea what it meant, but liked the way it sounded. We even curtailed our after work drinking and went home at 3:00am instead of 4:30 or 5:00. (Jerry slipped on a Wednesday shift so Huey and I had to remind him sternly of the vision.)

Early, on the Friday shift of the first week, Huey was reading the weather for Saturday which forecast 83 and humid, sunny. The ideas started to pass casually while I was pulling bottles in prep for the big happy hour. Thoughts of dinner once more, a show at Pianos, and crawling midtown all passed between us. Huey tried to press a day of drinking in the park, I said no twice and so he let it go.

Jerry Maxx had come up. He was just into his uniform, and he silently listened. I watched him fumble in casual movements knowing that he must have woken up just an hour ago, arrived to the coalmine, stood outside as he took hits off his one hitter, and finished with a Parliament.

"We should have our own liquor pull. Get a bunch of bottles and just have a night of it," Jerry Maxx said slowly looking himself over.

"Yeah, absolutely. Us, some bottles, some tranny hookers just off the Hudson," I said annoyed.

"No asshole…" he started calmly, "I mean a party with full bar and mixers. FULL bar and mixers."

"I understand what you mean. My point is, where? Cocksucker."

"We can do it at my place in Brooklyn," Jerry Maxx offered pouring himself a soda and enjoying it as if it were his last.

"In Bensonhurst? Who could get there?" I responded.

"Yeah. It's a ways, but get this, my roommate Ron is in Connecticut. We can probably do it at my place," Huey said wide-eyed and shrugging.

"On Park, huh? I always liked your place. Cozy, but just big enough," I said.

"Who the fuck names their kid Ron?" Jerry Maxx asked as he walked towards the kitchen solidifying that on 95th Street between Park and Madison the following night, our first Saturday with the three of us would be spent having a party with a full bar and mixers.

It was hot the next day most of which I slept through. I woke in a full sweat, the sun not so bright against the dirty yellow sheets I used as curtains. My roommate had left for work and by the freshly used shower smell in the hallway I imagined not too long before.

One From The Ice

As I walked to take a piss, the phone on the kitchen floor rang, and I knew that it must be Jerry Maxx. Huey rarely called.

"So what do we need, exactly?" he asked immediately and excited.

"What?"

"What do we need? You're the bartender. I've been callin' your ass for 45 minutes by the way! You need a fuckin' cell phone. I'm at the liquor store. What do we need?'

"What are you tuned up already?"

"No. That comes later. What do we need?"

"Ah, vodka, rum, gin, tequila, wait, you want tequila?"

"No. But I know broads get crazy on the shit."

"Yeah, they do. Ok, so let's do this, Absolut, Bacardi, 1800, Tanqueray, then pick up some simple things like triple sec, Apple Pucker, and like, Jaeger, or something to shoot. If it looks like we're gonna run out, then we'll make another run at a place by Huey's. I know a couple of spots over there. Oh! Powers. Get a bottle of Powers."

"What about like Scotch, or Kahlua? Or…"

"What are the Golden Girls droppin' by?"

"No. Listen, all I'm sayin' is, let's class some of this shit up. Let's get some Rusty Nails goin', let's get some SoCo, some White Russians, some Old Fashioneds, you know."

"You wanna do all that, cool. Keep the receipt though, and we'll divvy it up at Huey's. Who's comin' to this fuckin thing anyway?"

"Huey put the gentle word out, you know, not too many people, but there's obviously going to be some tail runnin' around the space."

"I'll call Alyssa."

"Yeah, cool. I guess I can call Texas Red."

"With or without his brother?"

"His brother's in Mexico, I think."

"Hopefully in a jail."

"Let me get goin."

"Wait. Who's on mixers?"

"Huey."

"Any food?"

"Such the wit."

"Seven-Thirty then?"

"Seven-Thirty."

I hung up the phone and doubted the entire thing. *Who the fuck's going to show to a house party in the middle of July?* I kept asking myself. In my

One From The Ice

bedroom, the digital clock on the edge of my bed read 3:45. I looked at the piece in progress on the easel. It had needed proper attention for weeks but I could not figure out in which areas. I did not need any more colors. My brushes were staring at me, well oiled, clean and ready soldiers blankly staring at their misguided, confused general. All the supplies I needed were perhaps a sandwich and definitely a bottle of God's whiskey and most of the night to figure it all out. But if I started then, I would ignore everything else. For days most likely. So I got in the shower as quickly as I could and damned the work.

At around 6:00pm as I stepped off the M96 at Park I recognized the pizza shop and the clean deli that always sold good cold beer. I went in and bought a twelve of Heineken and a twelve of Bud, and if anybody had a problem with those two *fuck 'em* I thought, it was more for me anyways.

I thought about my friend Alyssa having remembered to call her just before I left. She sounded excited when I asked her. She said in her soft NPR voice that she was going to bring her friend Natalie whom I never had met and perhaps Natalie's friend Janelle. It all began to sound promising even more so when Alyssa said that they were attractive and equally as ready for the Saturday night rendezvous. I had not been with a woman in sometime.

As I walked from 96th to 95th the 6:00pm sun was fading but holding onto every inch of its rays fighting with the last of its heat. The sweat really began to roll, the handles of the plastic bag were thin and twisted as I approached Huey's stoop. I wondered if the bags or I would make it up to the sixth floor. I decided to compose myself a moment before buzzing in. Cars drove casually and fluent in a weekend afternoon fashion. The playground across the street had six kids yelling in Spanish, laughing loud, and I noticed that the whole side of Huey's block was shaded, and that the playground was still beaming, the sun bouncing off the bright orange rubber of the slide and engulfing the deep yellow of a long tube that was blue at its highest end. I wiped the rest of the sweat as best as I could and rang the buzzer twice.

"Yeah?" Huey answered.

"Lady Bird Johnson for Pat Nixon."

"Get up here, tiger."

Taking several deep breaths, I decided just to attack the sojourn of the walk up. At the top, there was the prize, which got me through the first three flights calm and strong. Somewhere between three and a half and four my thigh muscles tightened, followed by slight gagging. My arms burned motionless, sweat pored from my forehead and stung my eyes. Finally, at the top I wished for better health and knocked weakly.

One From The Ice

The first after me to arrive was Jerry Maxx, on time and bitching. He brought with him in two large duffle bags all the bottles that I had said plus Drambuie, margarita mix, and a bottle of bitters all wrapped in newspaper that was wrapped by bathroom towels that he asked us to remind him about when he was going home. He mentioned everything was cheaper where he lived; therefore traveling with all those bottles all that way had made him quite thirsty. Huey smiled and rubbed Jerry's shoulders; I opened the bottle of Absolut and mixed him a large swallow with some ice tea, which was the only suitable mixer in the fridge. I noticed that we were going to need more ice, but I decided to keep my mouth shut until more people arrived, most assuredly one of them would be eager to help. Just as I finished my thought and my second sip of Bud, people started to arrive.

The first wave started with Danny Sullivan who worked the coalmines with us. He always wore a faded Mets cap, had a good deep laugh, and I noticed a couple of weeks beforehand that when he would get drunk he became cartoonish, sometimes violent. But walking in, Danny seemed in good spirits adding more beer to mine, a couple of extra packs of Parliaments for whoever wanted and a bottle of Ocean Spray.

Alyssa showed next, solid as her word with her two friends. She reminded us that we all had met Natalie before at a "Fine Wines" show, but as I glanced to Huey, then Jerry Maxx I knew none of us had remembered. She was attractive, thin, exotic looking with thick curls of black hair, olive skin, and eyes in a likeness of Cleopatra or some other Sanskrit drawing of women of that period. But she swore she was from Connecticut.

Janelle, who we all agreed that nobody had met, was a thicker blonde with California blue eyes. She seemed very pleasant, and I was immediately interested; however, she could not drop the ice she was carrying before Danny and Jerry Maxx were helping her and starting in on the small talk.

I looked to say hello to Alyssa who was unloading juice and soda with Huey. Instead of interrupting, I watched her fixed on Huey's every move smiling some moments before she caught herself. Sincere, casual right down to her sandals that were worn and brown, I thought of her as the girl on the street that all the mothers envisioned their boys with. Sand colored hair, green apple eyes, Alyssa already wore an end of August tan bronzed smooth and even across her skin, and all she probably did to get it was walk the streets. Jersey Shore girls always tanned the best.

Jerry Maxx' friend Heath stopped by shortly after the girls. I flat out did not like the bastard because I knew that he always carried a shit load of ecstasy and coke on him and that he was no smarter than two of

One From The Ice

my pubic hairs. He was a person of no character, and nothing to offer, yet would end up in some crevice or a shadow getting at least a blowjob. He was there for his drugs and who the hell was I to say one way or the other, so I shook his hand as firm as I did any other man's.

Immediately there was a polite buzz amongst everyone settling in. Jerry Maxx started to mix concoctions as if he knew what he was doing much to the delight of Huey and me. Alyssa asked if I was painting as much as I had been in the winter. I told her that I had calmed down but was planning to pick it up again and perhaps another show or "abomination" as I had started to refer to them after my November debacle in Dumbo. I sold one piece to an older homosexual gent in a hound's tooth coat. He wanted to commission me for some "work" at his townhouse in Park Slope, saying that I had a real Julian Schnabel quality. It soon became clear that the "work" would entail roller skates, wigs, and probably some Wham! tunes, their early stuff I imagined.

Midway through everybody's second round Texas Red showed up with his *Kid A* cd and a case of the Silver Bullet, which he pronounced as "kers light." After further inspection of the ole hoss, I noticed a 40 oz. of Country Club and two Philly cigars still wrapped. I pointed to all of it in an inquisitive gesture. He winked saying "You'll see. You'll see." I decided then that he was a very special personality, being raised in white-bred Texas, deciding for no reason to live in Harlem happier than he had ever been, and unharmed.

All of that spilled into conversation casual and unforced. Then when no one was looking, Huey slipped us a gift starting the night's music with Chicago's *Beginnings*, arranging the speakers outward, bobbing his head, smiling at me until I followed in unison.

"Listen to that sound----so fuckin' good. Those pure fuckin' horns," he said and the room listened for some moments.

By my fourth beer, Texas Red and Huey were in conversation over their mutual love for Central Park. It was interesting to listen to them talk about their completely different backgrounds, completely different habits, agreeing with pleasure and laughter of what they loved so much about Central Park. If they had been at a bar anonymously one was sure to make an ass out of the other. However, hearing Huey speak about the green of the Great Lawn, the spirituality of Strawberry Fields, the calmness amidst The Reservoir, gave way into Texas Red wiping his mouth with his forearm. Launching into his repertoire of walking from 110th Street to Columbus Circle, sometimes stopping for a couple of beers at Heckscher Field and watching the softball games. Other times he would smoke exactly two joints, take in the women or watch the disco roller skaters do their retro thing on Saturday afternoons.

One From The Ice

They caught me listening and asked what I loved about Central Park. I shrugged and said that I preferred Bryant Park to sketch commotion. They agreed I was full of shit and told me to fuck off.

Jerry Maxx was somewhere in between his fifth or sixth Rusty Nail saying that next time we should have cherries to properly garnish his new favorite drink. His white skin was starting to become flush in the shapes of tusks on the sides of his cheeks.

"My sister Lauren might show up," Jerry Maxx proclaimed in his thick Philly accent. "That should be a howl. You know she said she is really interested in seeing some of your work."

"Really?"

"Yup."

"Is she attractive?" I said smiling.

"Dude, you might be bigger than me, but you know what…"

"All right, take it easy. Take it easy." I knew right then that if she did show, I had a shot.

It was just dark and the whole room was sweating. The buzzer rang barely audible over the conversation and music. Huey answered standing by the door laughing and shaking his head. Jerry Maxx came from the bathroom wiping his nose, noticed me watching Huey, then noticed Huey almost doubled over, his hand on the door knob like a giddy butler using the mansion while his masters were away.

"Oh, it's her isn't it?! Jerry Maxx' eyes got wild as he ran his hand back and forth through his thick black hair that was beginning to take on a life of it's own in several different directions.

Drinking hefty swigs, I assumed it was Lisa, whom I had not yet met. A groupie of the highest order who would pursue Huey after shows, as aggressive and unabashed as a nineteen year-old Marine during Fleet Week.

"So you're a painter right?" Janelle said tugging unobtrusively at my wrist.

"Sometimes. I try." I responded, my blood filtering into insanity.

"Where did you study?" she asked with confidence.

"You're a painter yourself?"

"No. But I love art."

"Ah. A critic then?"

"No." She said, her face breaking into sarcastic smiles, her smell carrying over. A deep cinnamon scent, not floral as quite a bit of women use during the spring and summer, its full potential being held back by her sweat.

"Some of my influences are Van Gogh, Beckman, some DeKooning, Rockwell."

"Norman Rockwell?' she asked arching her back.

"Yeah. Stormin' Norman fuckin' Rockwell."

"Alyssa showed me some pictures of your last show."

"Ah yes. The abomination."

"It takes time."

"Thanks. What about you?"

"I work in an art gallery."

"Ah ha! Which one?"

"Soho."

"That narrows it. Which one?"

On cue to the hush of the crowd and before Janelle's answer, Lisa walked in with a bottle of Stoli Raspberry and a friend who Huey announced as Sarah. Jerry Maxx immediately blocked all views swallowing Lisa as if he had known her for years. I could not see her reaction, just her friend Sarah's wince of awkwardness much to Huey's delight.

When Jerry Maxx finally pulled back the first thing I noticed about Lisa was her thick, jet black Italian hair pulled back into a tight ponytail held in a white cloth hair band. She was almost as tan as Alyssa, a few pounds less heavy than Janelle, and it immediately struck me as curious as to how conservatively she carried herself while I recalled Huey's telling of all her indiscretions.

Her friend Sarah was hands down the most attractive woman in the room, and in five minutes, revealed the most unattractive personality in the apartment. Her red cut top was obviously expensive, as were her shorts, highlighted brown hair and maroon fingernails. I wondered how she knew Lisa, and if Lisa had come from such money. Sarah looked around as if she was asking herself what the hell was she doing in an apartment the size of her bedroom on a Saturday night.

When Huey introduced me to Lisa her thick brown eyes were shy and skeptical. Overly polite, she shook my hand lightly smiling as if we were in a boardroom at an office. I wanted to pull Huey aside right there to tell him he was full of shit about all the yarns he had spun about her. But he looked at me nodding as if I should just wait so I returned her politeness and ignored her friend Sarah.

One From The Ice

Further in, somewhere between *Evil Woman* and Jerry Maxx' impromptu solo rendition of *Psycho Killer* the conversations were heightened. The bottle of Absolut was empty, the Stoli Raspberry quickly became community property, Texas Red was pondering his first blunt at which point I alerted him that we were dangerously low on beer and that he should get more before lighting up to ensure the quality of the trip.

"How come I gotta go?" he asked with his chest cocked in defiance.

"Because I'm buying," I returned.

"Cool. I'll smoke me some trees en route. Maybe some on the way back, too."

"I'll go wit yas." Danny jumped in fixing his Mets cap for travel. I was glad to perhaps get some more time with Janelle as I handed three twenties to Red who winked at me like a teenager drunk for the first time.

As I walked over to her, Heath stopped me by the arm. He was speaking with Natalie who looked at me with interest so I obliged him and turned a shoulder into their conversation.

"You're a smart guy." Heath declared, and I shrugged. "Jerry's always saying how smart you are."

"I think interesting would be a better fit," I said sipping.

"Definitely interesting," Natalie said as if I were an uncle of whom she did not approve.

"What do you think of Giuliani?" Heath asked trying for Natalie's approval, and as I looked at the both of them, the only thing my mind found funnier than Heath's question was Natalie's genuine interest in him asking.

"I think that he got rid of a lot of homeless people," I said sipping, clearing a drip from the side of my mouth.

"Yeah, by dumping them into the East River," Natalie lashed.

"That's right." Heath agreed.

"You probably love the son of a bitch don't you?" she asked waiting to pounce.

"Love him? Not really, no. Son of a bitch, as you say, I wouldn't know."

"What about Dialla, or Dialyo, or, whatever the fuck....that guy," Heath fumbled.

"You mean, Amadou Diallo?" I asked.

"Whatever. Yeah."

"You think Mayor Giuliani personally ordered a hit on Amadou Diallou?" I asked.

"No, but his tactics sure the hell did," Natalie shot back.

"What tactics are those?" I asked.

"City wide police brutality. Do you live in a hole?" she asked looking across the room.

"You think Giuliani encourages murder and the tactics of police brutality?" I asked sipping.

"Hell yeah!" Heath exclaimed profoundly as Natalie nodded in agreement.

"Well…" I sighed looking at Heath's vacant eyes. "That's fucking atrocious."

"That's what we were just fucking saying!" he exclaimed half smiling.

"It's absolutely appalling. I feel so ashamed of New York City sometimes." Natalie sighed.

"Well…what are you guys going to do about it? I mean you two obviously feel very strongly about it, changes must be made, yeah?" I asked.

"What the fuck are WE gonna do about it?" Heath asked defiantly.

"Seriously. I mean, who's supposed to take on the cops and the mayor? Let alone us." Natalie said.

The thought to suggest that there were throngs of people who felt the same way protesting every hour of everyday fell to the wayside as I once again looked into Heath's soulless blue eyes and Natalie's perfect breasts peaking out of her white summer top. The conversation was just a pointless diversion until alcohol and drugs would give way to their real wants and concerns, and that seemed all American to me.

"Huh." I grunted. "I guess you're right."

Heath turned away for the bathroom most likely void of anything that had just occurred. Natalie stood there drinking something watered down by time and the heat, finally jumping onto another conversation with Janelle sitting alone. I found myself in the middle of the room equidistant to every huddle seemingly surrounding me.

Occasionally, Lisa talking to Sarah would catch my eye, her legs smooth and crossed. Alyssa had the ears of Jerry Maxx and Huey. Her lips moved faintly while her open outstretched palm went left to right describing something in the distance. Huey followed intently while Jerry Maxx wandered off disinterested.

One From The Ice

As much as I adored the three of them, and was every bit as much a part of their lives as they were mine, I was looking in as I had been doing most of my life. I knew that feeling when it enclosed me in the room amongst commotion and conversation. It was real, proven, and who I would always be, at least to some degree I thought. I knew at that point that I could live with it, where years earlier I would feel sorry for myself and question "why?" in pleading desperate maneuvers.

"MY FUCKIN' OLE MAN LOVES WOLFMAN JACK!!!" Jerry Maxx shouted. "Ah shit! c'mon Joycee, were sneakin' around with The Wolfman tonight!!!" He got up and stood over Lisa as she shook her head.

"My fucking mother loooooves The Wolfman…sorry." She said standing to take her ground.

"Not as much as my father, nope. Lisa, I like you, you're a good girl, but not for nothin' the ole bastard lives and dies on The Wolfman. I won't hear any more of it."

Huey came over to me laughing, rubbing my shoulders. I watched Alyssa get up to get another drink.

"Let's turn it up a bit," I said to Huey.

"Aaah yeah!" he agreed as he walked diligently to the stereo, and turned up *The Boy With The Arab Strap*. The sound came through crisp, clear. Looking around, everyone was into it, especially Alyssa; I knew it to be one of her favorites. Huey saw the same and fed off her, feeding it over to me simultaneously chiming in with the simple gorgeous hand clap layered in the background of the song.

"You can never go wrong with the hand clap!" Huey yelled out shaking one hand above his head in intervals as if he had a tambourine.

I lost track of what beer I was on thinking more and more of Janelle. The progression from just casual conversation was switching more prominently to physical thoughts of what kind of lover she was, what would she feel and taste like. Could she be as raucous as I? I decided on another beer, to further enhance these thoughts.

"Wanna bump?" Lisa asked grabbing my left hand, her low rasp clear, underneath all of the other noise as if she were Eve with an offering of fruit.

"Thank you, no. I can't go wrong with the beer," I said picturing how her body looked naked, and what her eyes reflected in the dark after just having sex. I almost yelled out for Huey to come over so that I could ask him dead to rights in front of Lisa why he had not taken every inch of her, but I let the moment pass.

One From The Ice

"Huey loves you." She said.

"I love him."

"I wanna see your shit. Can I see your shit sometime?"

"Of course."

"Are you having any fun here?"

"Loads."

"Cocksucker." She said blankly.

"Whore." I said on edge.

"Finally! Somebody in this fuckin' forsaken room who gets it!" She kissed me on my neck and walked away.

We were flying high. Every one of us seemed to have nice thick buzzes. Lisa now was openly making oral offerings to Huey, and when Huey would laugh and shake his head she would turn to Jerry Maxx who would be whispering offerings in her ear, and the two would make out, sip, and make out some more. Their hands eventually forgot that anybody was around, or cared. The view of the whole scene danced around the room as if it came from a dirty Fitzgerald dream. It started out as just another mad act of Jerry Maxx twisting and writhing, turning legitimate when Huey joined, followed of course by Alyssa during the climax of the Commodore's *Machine Gun* right through ELO's *Showdown*. Then even the queen Sarah rose to meet the challenge on *Jive Talkin'*.

It was more than just drug addicts and rummies. It was a throwback to Saturday night and how the inception of its rituals at some point had come about naturally. It was our Saturday night, and as I watched the room move, I did not see it as idiots in a trailer trash bar in Florida, or as cheese dripping from a disco ball as it watched the electric slide. I saw it as a natural course of pure joy that I had not previously witnessed, not a phony smile in the house.

When the dancing subsided, everyone was sweating and flush. Huey suggested the roof, in thinking about it for the first time. I was the last one through an old staircase lined with paint cans and a couple of two by fours as near as I could tell. Texas Red and Danny Sullivan had spent most of the night on broken lawn chairs as we found out. They were quite high, and very drunk. Sullivan saw Janelle and again went straight for her. Closer in I could see she was not having any of it, much to Texas Red's amusement.

I was double fisting, not wanting to go back and forth. The air on top was cooler than the apartment, yet still warm enough to be July. I wondered how long we could get away with being up there. The mood was still of excitement though carrying itself more subdued in a "wait and see" manner. The crowd to my surprise was less sloppy than I had anticipated them being at that point in the night. I kept one eye on Sullivan waiting for his switch to turn to "messy." But as several moments passed that must have led to about an hour later, there seemed to be no complaints, no fights, or vomit, and Sullivan curled up on the warm asphalt arms wrapped around a chimney.

The snob Sarah left as phony as she came saying that she had another party to attend before going home. Texas Red took one of the longest pisses I had ever seen, on another building top just over a three foot partition before disappearing. Per usual, Heath went for a "walk" with Natalie, leaving Alyssa, Huey, Janelle and me, which was just about perfect leaving hope a flame in the night.

Janelle started to ask me about my work again, and I told her I really was not interesting enough to hold a conversation about it. We moved onto her saying that she liked New York well enough, but could only see herself here another year or so, while going on about how great Chicago was. I nodded and added that Walter Payton was one of my favorite athletes of all time and she returned a blank look with a semi nod. At that point, I switched the conversation to her current romantic involvements. She smiled politely and invited Huey and Alyssa into the fold.

"Bye, bye lady." I muttered.

I walked over the partition where Texas Red went to piss. "Hey, where are you going?" Alyssa said.

"To piss, I'll be right back," I said with no intention of going back, at least not immediately. I put my empty bottle down and smiled at my full one. I saw the lake that Texas Red had left and stepped over and to the left of it to create my own. When I was done, I noticed that Janelle was not there, and I watched Alyssa hang on every gesture of Huey's, the two of them perched on the concrete ledge over looking 95th Street. I thought about how she had turned me down weeks earlier. Then I thought about Jerry Maxx and Lisa in Huey's roommate's bed, probably having good and dirty sex, then I wished I played the guitar, how I believed in Huey's rock-n-roll, trying on a smile thinking about Jerry Maxx' unabashed brass balls.

I eyed the dark asphalt with a rusted out Weber Grill next to one of the other chimneys, and a two-legged table on its side, the type my father would break out in setting up for Thanksgiving, Christmas, and Easter. Across the park, against grey night there was an outline of a water tank, further beyond that were outlines of high rises uneven, overlooking the East River that I was sure was there, although I could not see it. Then the phrase "one day" came and went several times.

One From The Ice

The roof top door slammed open cutting into everything settled in. I was sure it was the cops, or a neighbor. Emerging was Lisa wrapped in a white comforter, Jerry Maxx naked, his arms around her, his mouth still in her ear, and up and down her neck.

"Huey!" she yelled. "Are you coming to bed?!"

Sean Welsh

UNCLE TOM'S SAAB

She was nice enough I thought as I walked over damp sidewalks, breath faint, stomach full. I was content to know my next love, my next relationship would not be with her, and I did not care about having spent $300.00 for a fine meal. It was as if I had been looking at something as gorgeous as a Coltrane horn, and all it would play symbolized beige wallpaper over a slow, dry, wind brazen death in the Gobi. On Sixth Avenue the soldiers were still atop the marquee at Radio City, and the traffic was not quite back to normal. The climate was still settling from the silly season, bracing for two months of winter marching towards St. Paddy's.

Where would the next one be? I was tired of hookers and pleasure brats. What small crack or shadow would embrace my heart again? Did I really even want it? Probably not ready for it. *Shut up*. I told myself. I came to remembering my first, and then further beyond, all the way back to the Saab.

Uncle Tom would show up on birthdays, sometimes Christmas...always with different women, always with the best gifts, the best laugh, and stay for the shortest time. He would kick me cash against the old man's wishes and spoke to me as a friend about young ladies,

One From The Ice

music, his experiences and what he learned about doing things right, the latter of which I would not learn myself for some years. Uncle Tom then, and to this day wore a smile up to his eyes that were my grandmother's green. He laughed in sentences and smoked Barclay's. The shift and snap of his Zippo, his first exhale was better than the aromas of a bakery, especially embedded into the leather of his Saab.

It was the first sports car in my family that I could recall at the time. My ole man used to gloat about a Mustang he had when I was three, but I could never recall it. After years of school, just in time for the days of *Miami Vice* and yuppiedom, Uncle Tom scored a traveling gig selling hospital equipment, and the company vehicle he chose was a black Saab.

Remembering it all now, I was not initially impressed. It was not Mark Jenna's cousin's Vette with the orange atmospheric paint job, side pipes, and moon roof. It didn't even have the muscle mystique and credibility of Tommy Farnsworth's blue Camaro, who lived across the street. Granted, the Camaro was as cool as they come, but even cooler because it was Tommy's, and he used to be a Green Beret.

It was not until an afternoon while we were heading to the Knick's game that Uncle Tom played mixed tapes on the Clarion stereo with its adjustable equalizer. Speeding down the Saw Mill to the West

Side Highway, commanding the five speeds as if he invented them, constantly adjusting the beeps on his Passport detector with the smell of hundreds of dead and smoked Barclay's cured into the leather of the dash and seats, the Saab 900 Turbo rose above all else. On the street amongst my friends it was a shoulder shrug of an "eh." But I kept it to myself, that special place inside, the summer nights when he would grease me his keys.

    Those first summer nights that would represent many, Uncle Tom wanted some privacy with the ole man and could not get it with me persisting that *Bobby Jean* was the best cut on *Born in The USA*. (Which it is.) Slick as he was, he showed me that the big key with the rubber end did everything. He slowly, quietly demonstrated how to turn away from the dash counter clockwise so as to bypass the alarm. Once I was inside, to lock up immediately and to absolutely stay away from the gearshift and safety break jackknifed upwards just beyond the arm rest. The ignition was to be turned one click forward, not more, because he didn't want my ole man to have to give him a jump, and if that happened, he and I both would be in "hot shit." By doing all this, the Clarion should be played at a "Go nuts level." Later on as it became ritual, he asked that the equalizers be returned to his settings. This made sense to me because I would have wanted the same.

One From The Ice

Inside, I locked the door immediately. The steering wheel was thick, the Saab crest dead center. The key went in as I had seen him do three or four times before, one click forward, the green lights breathed life in the equalizer below, but not the stereo, and my blood raced. What did I do? What did I do? Should I go and get him? I wanted it to be perfect. Eyes wide, I reached for the large knob on the stereo face and turned it on with hope.

Jimmy Buffet came through, and so I immediately ejected the tape. It exited after a slight pause and a sound familiar to something on a *Star Trek* episode. I put it into its proper case upon opening the arm rest revealing all the tapes he had made and bought, all the tapes he traveled with all over the country, and I sat not knowing where to begin…content to start in silence. It was me getting ready to drive, I was tall enough, in that seat it became my Saab, my tapes, the cigarettes smelled so rich, the beige of the leather was barely visible in the night under the shadow of the tree just before the orange and hum of the streetlight above.

They were the days of Tom Petty's *You Got Lucky* and Billy Squire's run that ran into J. Geils, ZZ Top, and Foreigner. Just before Van Halen's rise, just before Pat Benatar's decline, Squeeze and John Waite, Prince, some Hall and Oates with glimpses of Rush, The Honeydrippers, and whatever the Stones were doing. Every twenty minutes you could hear *Jack And Diane* on at least two stations, and the "Pink Houses" contest on MTV where a then John Cougar would come for a barbeque.

    The summers bread a comfort and a Catholic child's shame. Her breasts were pointed, and showed veins streaking their sides. She took her bra off, and I sucked them apprehensively at first, as my birth rite later. I imagined myself pulling in front of her house in the Saab, my hand gently palming the gearshift, lazily swaying it from side to side in neutral, waiting with confidence.

    She would run slightly, then saunter. Everybody would be watching and when she was in, my hand would feather us into first, dip us into second, jam us into third. As I made a right she would hold my hand, and the blood would rush up through my cheeks when she would lean over and put her tongue against mine, just as she had taught me to do to her.

    I resigned to the radio at first just to break the silence. Both windows were cracked slightly allowing June gusts to relieve some of my sweat. On the dial country, classical, college, rock, oldies. I was strictly rock-n-roll with an occasional flip to the oldies for some origins, Del Shannon, Van the man, or anything meeting criteria of that grit and soul.

One From The Ice

The night was limitless, serene, holding all of its passion very guarded, gently waiting for me stumbling in it…new. There was no pressure inside the Saab; it was me flying vivid with sight and conviction though the Saab did not move from the curb. He had cassettes of greats that I heard, but was not "hearing" at the time. Tull, Santana, Goodbye Yellow Brick Road. I dabbled with Bowie but would not fully understand until years later when I would first be getting drunk on the weekends. Usually the day after these nights I would wake up late, eat my peanut butter toast, and go to the pool late. Everyone would always wonder where the hell I was…this night I was driving there.

When I park outside the fence the white of the lights high above will sink into the black of the water. We'll sit on the hood, as if we were lifeguards, Dave and his girl, only I'll have the Saab and Dave's girl will want me then as well. Just like little Maria down the street who will be gorgeous one day and likes me very much but has no breasts and kisses hard with no tongue. Or perhaps Viv Maloney who looks like a willing pale sex goddess in her blue Speedo one piece until she stares at me with her droopy eyes and a smile her parents cannot yet afford to fix. None of them was Carol Kintana.

Gliding down the West Side Highway, a knot in the stomach just over the slight rise and dip around 95th Street, night and everything in it, fifth gear undisturbed until the docks where the ocean liners sleep as they wait to shove off. Maybe, to pick up Rick Rodriguez, the all-state catcher and his girl, the all-state beauty, the all-cool kid in the all-cool Saab with sexy Carol K.

The reality of my father in the house talking about how shitty my grades were for that year was gone. His impending decision on sending me to summer school, taking away mid-afternoons of freedom and the pursuit of Carol's body now were superfluous. Confidence rode the moonlight and shined through the speakers.

If the Arthur Avenue boys wanted to start any shit I was ready. I'd whip this fucking fist right into the heart of anything meaningful, and everybody around would talk in whispers as I drove away. Manhattan never saw anything like me. The Man With No Name in the *Dollars' Trilogy*, John Milner in his piss yellow deuce coup, Eddie Wilson wandering a haunted boulevard.

After I showed them, Dad would not care about my grades, or what my friends and I did in secret places around the neighborhood. Making out in the bushes after dark, exploring new avenues that were our bodies under the shadows of "sleepovers" massive block-long games of

One From The Ice

"tag" and block parties, while our parents drank beer and boxed wine, listening to 50's and 60's juke box music.

I wanted Carol to be my girl, and only mine. Her brother Jayson, with his confident blonde hair, told me of all the other ones she kissed, and I would stop him when he elaborated. I thought about her tongue in my mouth, and what she taught me. I took to kissing Viv Maloney in the same fashion, and it was not the same. Though her body still damp from the Speedo was full and arousing, I would not have wanted Viv in the Saab.

Orange streetlights one after the other standing guard through streets that would dip and jag. The West Side Highway looping to the FDR, Canal Street to Seventh Avenue, around Battery Park to the Fish Market…windows down.

His tapes were not arranged in any order, and he handwrote the titles and contents which forced me to hold them to as much light as I could from the outside, not even thinking of turning on the dome light. It was where I belonged and the start of many nights for which I would practice. They were visions created by swirling spirits of contentment, rushed romance and strokes of real confidence. The night created more soul than the day, thus providing more cover to kiss and feel, giving desperation and meaning to the music, undisturbed and boundless in the Saab.

I found myself still walking at age 32 at 43rd and Sixth. It was cold, my eyes were watering down my face, and my nose was sore from wiping it. I caught a cab to Queens and pondered a nightcap.

One From The Ice

WARM AND DRY

It was just night, raining and cold when he slammed the cab door in her face on Canal Street four blocks fresh from the Manhattan Bridge. She told the cab driver to pull two blocks ahead of him and drop her on the corner in front of the old dim sum shop now closed. In two years they will be broken up. A year later she will not want to know him. This night, the sharpness of what she had to do was never clearer. Embedded in her subconscious, it was becoming second nature as a soldier amongst fire exchange, holding a fierce determination and a belief in being a part of something bigger than herself fighting against the end.

Standing under a $3.75 umbrella that she brought with them to the party, that he said that they would not need, she spotted him swaying a bit. People were moving to avoid him, and as he passed her, she heard him shouting to himself angrily, on his way to becoming unwittingly soaked.

Some further thoughts of leaving him to roam ran not just through her mind, but through her body all the way to her feet poised on her toes that moved in the direction of their Upper West Side apartment. But what if he would need her? What if he was to get into a fight or smacked by a cab? What if he was to be arrested for something embarrassing? What if he were to pick up a stray woman at one of those filthy dives he would resort to? She had to stay and make sure. She decided that there would be plenty of time to be mad in the morning, perhaps the week if she felt.

Following from at least six heads back, she thought about what she said and what she did at the party. Maybe she pushed him so hard to stop drinking that he drank harder to spite her. "His friends. His goddamn friends," she said underneath her breath, the shadow of her words outlined in tufts of air underneath the lights.

She saw simple signs of the trouble, feeling them into fruition in the pit of her stomach as they happened. He did not eat, and there had been plenty to go around. It was the slow glazing of his eyes, a multitude of shots, and the short time in which he downed them. The height of his happiness, his arm around her, kissing her with forced compliments, forced by the rivers of alcohol floating in his veins. She stood next to him smiling.

Perhaps it was the "tough guy" mantras that would usually follow on the way down that sent her into a mission to get him out of there. He was big, but his mouth when he was that way was bigger, and more wicked people than he was she felt, had been sizing him up over their

One From The Ice

shoulders, indirectly out of the corners of their eyes, the way she had seen other times just before the trouble would happen.

Crossing Broadway, the rain had let up to a mist. The Crate And Barrel lit up his body, and she could see clearly that he was on his phone yelling in spurts, his left arm flailing in harsh rhythms. *Christ knows who he called, and God help them* she thought. Her feet damp on just the top, she smiled to herself on her choice of shoes.

He made a right on Mercer heading towards the park. Mercer was quieter than she remembered at that point. Only a few shops and a dirty restaurant were open on the block, and there were just a couple of bodies separating them now as she slowed down, moving to her right, so as not to lose total sight of him, so as not to be caught.

His voice began to carry, bouncing off the buildings, sometimes being washed out by intermittent traffic. She moved closer to listen, catching him shouting, cursing, then quiet, listening, shouting again. It was just before crossing West Third that she clearly heard her name, followed by "she." A cold shake went through her throat down into her thighs.

"Can't fuckin' stand it anymore! Fuckin' bitch! It was a goddamn party!!! What the fuck?!!" Silence. "Don't fuckin' tell me to calm down! You fuckin' sound just like her!!!"

She assumed it was his brother Danny as she conjured up images of him last Christmas unable to walk from drink and his very young girlfriend Heather, sloppily helping him to bed.

"Fuck it! I'll stay with Tom! You know something, you're either with me or against me, kid! Yer fuckin' crazy, out of the question, yer fuckin' crazy. Fuck her!!! What did I fuckin' do?!...Ah, the Village, I think."

He slumped down against the gate of a nail shop carelessly animated on the way to the sidewalk. One of his legs was straight out, and she could see the Skechers she bought him scuffed with no regard. She felt silly spying on him in the streets that she knew better than he did. What would her father think of all of it if he could see the scene? Her lover's dismal caricature drawn to a drunken puddle, a sewer away from his talents and what she was in love with.

"I don't fuckin' know. I dunno where she fuckin' is…home…I dunno. I'm a fuckin' man for Chrissakes! What? Fuck that! I could take care of my fuckin' self! I'm not yelling at you bro, I'm just fucking pissed. I could fuckin' care less. I'm done with this bullshit here. Yeah well, you don't have to live with her. I'm not even that fuckin' bad, just a little buzzed."

One From The Ice

She began to try and grind into herself that he did not mean any of it. Waiting for him to say anything else she could see his eyes open and shut lazily. Moving his phone from ear to ear to try and stay awake, she moved one to two feet back, then closer depending upon which way his head swiveled, and which way the people came and went, some of them just stepping over him.

"Okay bro, okay, alright, yea, love you too."

He used the gate to pull himself up scaring her to move when he almost fell into the street looking for a cab. There were none. He looked back at one point causing her to think he spotted her, maybe ignored her. But, she reasoned that the depth of shade she watched from was good enough and watching him stumble further she doubted he could notice anything a foot in front of his face.

A cab passed her after several touch and go moments stopping for him, pulling away just as quick. To her luck, another approached just seconds later and when she spoke to give directions to follow him, it was replaced by directions to their apartment. "Please take Tenth Avenue to 81st and Amsterdam," she said soft, tired.

She took out her phone to call her sister *and say what?* She hesitated. Her sister would know that something had gone down, and she never lied to her sister. Further what would her sister say? To end it. It was not nearly the first or second time, just the first time she trailed him, hearing him that way. Then what would her sister say about that? To end it quickly in a raised voice that her sister would get whenever she felt threatened. Sister would not understand, not yet, the wonderful deep emotions and life they shared outside of situations such as this night. And the question of 'how many more nights…' was not even a relevant question. She weighed what he said against how she still felt, how she knew and believed he felt about her and put her phone away.

    She did not realize how wet she was until she sat some moments in the dry cab. The back heater fluttered, barely working just enough to make the ride home better than the subway. She rested motionless swaying with stops, absorbing potholes, rises, dips, and turns wishing 17th Street into 10th Avenue, praying for 10th Avenue to become Amsterdam. She wanted the rain to turn to snow so she could watch it quietly from their bedroom window looking out onto 81st Street just before the corner where the dry cleaner was.

    The cab pulled to 81st, she asked to stop at the near corner. Looking across Amsterdam to their building, she thought she saw a glimpse of him disappear into the light of the doorway. She wanted no confrontation and tried to kill time by making small talk with the driver

One From The Ice

while fumbling for her money that she usually always had ready. She left abruptly when he started to come on to her.

The rain had started again as she wondered who was working the door and what state her drunkard was in at this point. Their sushi spot was just closed, the gate not completely shut. The bodega had no signs of gang bangers out in front, and through their open window where the Pakistani owners took money for their newspapers, she heard their Arabic mixed with their laughter. The old church was standing behind her dark, quiet, and further thoughts of waiting it out on its short set of stairs were quickly washed with tiredness, and her final feelings of being too cold to stand any more of it, come what may.

"Oh, no Missus! My oh my! What did you do to that boy?! My oh my."

It was Eugene, her favorite, working the door, just sitting down. She knew he had probably just helped him up, as he had done before.

"Yea." She shook her head quietly.

"I ain't never seen him like that! Worse than the last time even!"

She reached in her damp purse for a twenty as she had the last time, the time before in thanks for his troubles. But, Eugene stood up shaking his head, waving a hand, putting it on her wrist, his skin warm and coarse.

"Nah honey, not this time. Get some rest. Yous had yas' hands full all night I's imagine."

She nodded her head, he sat down watching her to the elevator. Walking she heard his light jazz being turned up combined with the warmth of the lobby, she could have stayed there for another few minutes. Her mind for the first time all night was relaxed.

She softly, cautiously opened the door though she felt quite confident that he was passed out. She spotted his shoes strewn stride after stride and a book lying face down between them. His snoring followed next, swallowed by a siren running up Amsterdam. She put her purse on the table. She hung up her jacket, put her shoes by the door, took off her socks and her jeans, stepping over his shoes and the book, leaving them for evidence.

The overhead light in their bedroom was bright. He was face down on the bed, the cuffs of his jeans sopped, his jacket half off. Sighing she took her jeans, socks, and threw them on top of the laundry bag. She did the same with her bra and panties, putting on her Yankee sweats and N.Y.U. hoody. She turned on the television and walked to the bathroom.

One From The Ice

Her hair was still damp and would not dry for hours. She ran the water warm, and used the gentle cleanser he had gotten her for her birthday, putting the lather and water deep into her skin over and over. She grabbed the white towel she had hung from the fresh laundry bag she forced him to finally go and get earlier in the afternoon. She planted her face in it for several moments and breathed in its cleanliness, it's soft fabric.

In the bedroom she turned the overhead light off, then turned the lamp on her side of the bed on, just one click. The wood of the floor was warm, the radiator clanking, beginning to hiss in the corner. He had not moved.

It took all of her strength and several soft grunts to turn him over and rip his jacket off from beneath him. Undoing his jeans, she pulled them down once from the top as much as she could, then finishing with another full strength tug that almost sent her into the computer behind her at the foot of their bed. He lay there with drool on the side of his cheek as she took his socks off, leaving him there in his blue striped boxer briefs and black Calvin Klein button down that her mom had gotten him for his birthday.

"Idiot." She sighed.

She got under the covers next to him and grabbed the remote next to the lamp on her side of the bed. Her mind was blank, happy to be watching Sunday night television. Happy he was home and passed out. Happy to be in their bed under the flannel sheets and thick comforter, warm and dry.

CUSTOMS

Save for perhaps an Indian summer, summer was gone. We were coming off of a good one, a full one, but from the periodic deep sighs of everyone in the back garden, happy to see it go. The leaves had just started to turn and our dress was different. My father had his traditional Irish wool, my brother Dave had a brown Phat Farm sweatshirt with the hood pulled over. Uncle Ike had a burgundy turtleneck, and I had a black one.

"Man that was great meat, Ike." Dad said sitting back.

"Yeah. Not too shabby. My guy does a nice job." Uncle Ike took out four cigars from his breast pocket, handed three to Dad who passed us the other two.

"Where's this guy now?" I asked as I unwrapped it, not even looking at the brand because it did not matter; they were good because they were Uncle Ike's.

"Who? The butcher?" he asked spitting the tip into the tomato bed.

"Yeah," I responded spitting my tip over the fence into the Jesus lovers' yard next door.

"Bob Reyes. Dominican guy. His shop's in Inwood. Good story this guy…" Uncle Ike paused to light taking several deep puffs until that distinctive smell clouded his face. Then as he held the cigar to the side he handed Dad the thick lighter only used on occasions. We all followed suit and listened.

"This guy, comes over in a cargo plane, I shit you not, bolted into a four by six crate that his uncle put him in. His uncle owned some sort of citrus, or sugar, or whatever they export down there. Anyways, I guess things got a little tight with the policia and his uncle. I guess there was a new chief that wanted a piece of the business, but they wouldn't give it up, some bullshit, I don't know. Anyways, they kill his mother, his uncle's sister, and Bob was next unless, well, you know."

"What about his father?" Dave asked.

"Don't know. Never came up. Anyways, Bob almost dies of malnutrition in this fucking crate you know. The crate gets delivered to a butcher who was friends with Bob's uncle on the South Shore. They get him to a hospital, adopt him, Bob takes over the business, moves it to Inwood." Uncle Ike shrugged and puffed matter of factly.

"How old was he when they shipped him?" Dad asked calmly.

"Six, seven something like that."

"Has he ever been back?" I asked looking at my cigar.

"Once, I think," Uncle Ike, said licking his lips.

"The uncle?" Dad asked.

"Oh, who the hell knows? Shit, I don't quite believe the whole thing's true anyways. I just tell it because his meat's so goddamn good."

Mom was tucked away inside, and her shadows would sometimes overcast onto the dying lawn with a vanilla orange background from the dining room. We knew she was not coming out, at least for some time, and I felt free to talk amongst everybody, excited, eager but patient.

"Feels good," Uncle Ike said. We all nodded.

The air breezed and my snot ran thinner and quicker causing some slight sniffles. I puffed, the cigar smoke was thicker in the crisp air; the early grey of the sunset watched over the four of us. I sat for the first time in a long time not needing a bar, not looking to get to the shore late night, not needing to move.

"How's the city?" Uncle Ike asked me. I took a minute, huffing.

"It's nice," I said licking my lips.

"How's Bitch Sox town?" I asked after a pause.

"Only three back," he said puffing.

"Three enough." I retorted.

"How'd the trip in treat ya' Ike?" Dad asked.

"Beautiful actually. I love the train."

"What'd ya' rent a Lincoln?" Dave asked.

"No, uh uh. I went with the Sebring."

"How's it ride?" Dad asked looking over.

"Nice," Uncle Ike said puffing. "Really well."

"You know we would have came and got you from the station," Dad threw in.

"Nah. This way nobody skips a beat. I like to drive the city and the turnpike any way."

"Well gentlemen, how 'bout the hooch?" Dad asked calmly.

"Please," Dave said hopefully.

"Shut up. You can go and get yourself a soda," Dad said walking by, slapping the side of his head. Uncle Ike and I sat smoking in changes of breezes, and I tried to think about something other than baseball to talk about, but could not. On the table in the middle of it all were a bottle of Jameson's and a bottle of Johnny Walker Black that Uncle Ike brought trimmed with three glasses and a six of Heineken for Dad and I to wash all of it down. Uncle Ike drank straight, Dave had a can of Coke, and I thought about mixing my first Jamey down with a splash, but the ole man would have slapped me upside the head, and I did not feel like enduring it in front of Uncle Ike. I was with men now, I thought to myself, in toe, following their lead. Dad cracked both bottles, and poured healthy doses, then handed me a beer as he sat back and relit his cigar.

"Uncle Ike, you worked security?" I asked sipping my whiskey, sipping my beer.

"When I retired from the force I hooked a job for a major law firm who did a lot of foreign affairs and government work. I did their security, yeah."

"That's where all of the traveling came in?" I asked.

"Eighty percent, yeah."

"The other twenty?" Dave asked grinning.

"None of your goddamn business," Uncle Ike said.

"Ike, where was the scariest place you ever traveled to?" Dad asked.

"Well…" He moved, readjusting his legs, sipping then puffing full of thought. "I'm not quite sure about the scariest, but Nicaragua in the early mid-eighties certainly comes to mind." He took another sip; Dave and I sat up.

"Yeah. I was told to go down there and scout hotels, eateries, all that shit cause they were sending down a partner and a couple of associates for…some bullshit, I don't know. But, Nicaragua, for you younger gents, was pretty heavy with action back then. It was one of my first jobs, I didn't know shit, but the pay was more than substantial so, fuck it, what are ya gonna do right? So, my Español was non-existent. All I knew were a couple of words, and it's hard to blend in and be a non-obtrusive tourist with your weapons blazing just to get a towel, so once I pointed my way to the hotel and town that I had to do surveillance on, I hired this guy from the hotel who was like their concierge to be my escort for about three weeks. Wasn't my money, I didn't give a shit, help this kid out meantime right?" We all nodded.

"Well, midway through the stay I'm pissed off. Food sucks, I can't sleep because I got one eye on the door all night. I'm the only white motherfucker in the country who's not Agency, I couldn't even blend in to have a cup of coffee. Everybody knows what I am by this time; I decide to get drunk. I'm here to tell you…you hear about Mexican and Turkish prisons, couldn't shit in the direction of where I ended up." He

One From The Ice

shot the bottom quarter of his drink and waved Dad off reaching for another.

"I broke three knuckles and resorted to tactics of early manhood. I used dirt to wipe my ass and only because of my early days, thank Christ for all those silly Saturdays of tae kwon do, did I get to eat. I vowed to kill every lawyer if I survived and to personally fund the deconstruction of the country. Would you believe gentlemen…" he paused sipping, "that I was only in for three days."

"What sprung you?" I asked.

"They searched my wallet and found a picture of me shaking hands with Dennis Martinez…the pitcher. I was working in Baltimore for a year and got to meet him. I kept it in there for a joke. They asked me if I knew him, I lied and said that the firm represents him…they let me out. Gave me a fuckin' ride to the airport. Cock suckers."

"What'd you tell the firm?" Dad asked.

"That the country's not safe."

"What'd you do to get locked up?" Dave asked.

"Can't remember. They never told me. My objective at that point was to get out. I send El Presidente an unmarked fruit basket every year on his birthday. You know how hard it is to find and ship a fruit basket in June?"

It got a little chillier, but the only one it affected was Dave who I caught shivering. I thought for sure within the next couple of minutes as the three of us sipped and sat that Dave would leave for the house. He did not, and I was glad. I looked back, and the vanilla orange of the kitchen light was gone, and I envisioned Mom concerned about us reading her book.

"I cannot tell you how lucky we have it here in the U.S. People, millions of people, live, crawl, survive, die, like animals…literally. We're lucky. At our worst, we still have it the best."

"Well, Ike, let's change gears, where'd you have the most fun?" Dad asked.

"New Zealand. By far and away, New Zealand. One hundred and eighty degrees from what I just said, New Zealand. Brochures do it no justice. I am going to do it no justice by trying to relay it to you, New Zealand…I don't know. Timing has a lot to do with it."

"The women?" Dave asked, and it was on my mind too.

"The women in New Zealand? Or the most beautiful women I have seen?"

One From The Ice

"Most beautiful," Dave said

"Well, now you're talking Argentina. Argentinean women are the most beautiful, yes. And I'll tell ya something; they retain it just as well. Very greedy, though. They're always looking to trade up with their looks for something more. Crazy too, but all women are nuts." He put his cigar on the edge of the table and sipped healthy.

"I brought a lady back from one of my trips down there, just for the hell of it. Mistake. I was living on the Upper West Side, nice place on 96th and West End. From the time she met one of the doormen to the time she left you could see her trying to find a way to stay, to use me, the doorman, anything. Abril was her name. I was in a real mess with her because I liked what she did for me but on the other end, completely draining."

"High maintenance," I said.

"Not worth it, is more like it," Uncle Ike said.

"Whatever happened to Becca, Ike?" Dad asked.

"I gave up because she didn't like my drinking habits, and I agreed because she drove me mad cap." He crossed his legs at the ankles looking into what was left of the sky, sighed, and took a drink.

"What'ya gonna do?" he muttered to Dad.

Dad sat still, still puffing slightly, nodding his head, looking straight.

"Was she the one?" Dave asked.

"The one what?" Uncle Ike retorted.

"The one you would tell us about bringing us to the fish market?" Dave asked spitting to his side.

"Absolutely." Uncle Ike said pointing at Dave.

Dad tried to cover all of it with ridiculous politeness, but after that was over the three of us resorted into pissing into driveways and gardens sometimes not our own. Dave laughed at us and sipped whiskey while our backs were turned. I knew that he did because that's what I used to do, because that's what they let me do, and for the first time I was pissing along side the big boys.

One From The Ice

CHECKMATE

Johnny Faith I used to call him due to the fact that he had none. His real name was John Leo Delaney. We worked together at an office supply company called Checkmate on Forty-Fourth Street and Eleventh Avenue. Johnny was in charge of their shipping and receiving and ran his operation in the "gray." Meaning getting things done, but not in the least bit the way the company set up or intended. But Johnny's ways were cost efficient, effective, thus as always in business, blind eyes were turned.

I started at Checkmate in August of which year I cannot recall. It was hot and where I was assigned as the new guy hotter, even Johnny had no A.C. in his office, just a small oscillating fan that he called "Tits." Sometimes "Tits" would get thrown into the glass, onto the dock, kicked, punched, spat on, taped up, ignored and put away however remaining for the duration of Johnny's tenure.

Johnny was short, muscular with no fat to spare. He wore glasses more often than not, his hair was rust colored, and his skin was freckled Irish white. Most of the guys were two and three times his size, but no matter how hard he rode them they rarely bitched, taking care of their orders and responsibilities as a proud cohesive crew. It helped that

Johnny was one of them, Jersey Irish Catholic, which was what I was, and in looking back, probably a chief reason as for my hiring.

Usually on the onset of starting a new job (I had quite a few back then) guys would warm up to me pretty quick. I could recite most baseball and football facts, stats, as well as opinions and insights…only when asked. I was on time, never called out, never had a woman, or women hanging around or calling for me. If you pressed me as it tends to happen, and you were wrong you heard about it, and in just a handful of instances you felt it. Johnny did not know my face for two months; he did not learn my name until the end of the third. *Better off*, I thought.

As time came to pass, the work pace thickened. I started to care more about the job than learning who Johnny really was. For that bubble the politics evaded me. I clocked in, I clocked out. My sweat was as thick as the guys around me. I bought a decent bed for a decent one bedroom in Woodside. Once a month I would take a friend to Luger's, on Fridays I would meet some old friends downtown, on Saturdays I would have burgers at Donovan's and then try to pick up at Saints and Sinners, Sean Ogg's, Toucan Tommy's, or The Starting Gate. It all agreed with me the way a young drinker's life should agree with him. Somewhat regimented with solid people and a place to cover up when it was done.

One From The Ice

Late October on a Friday night I was sweeping some packaging from the floor of the dock. It was a half an hour from punch time, and I was thinking about looking up a secretary from Ernst and Young who said she would be at her happy hour spot in the Thirties by Penn Station. I kept thinking about kissing her full Dominican lips, then what her body, thick and firm, would feel like in my hands, which led to thoughts about how clean my sheets were.

"McKenna!"

Johnny stood in front of his office flanked by Ralphy Boy Sherman and Pat Raymond. Decent enough guys whom I heard would not be there after Christmas.

"You Yankees or Mets?"

"Yankees." I said dumping the paper into the dumpster.

"Told ya." Ralphy Boy yelped rubbing his slight belly.

"Well how the fuck should I know? He works like a Mets guy...I still think he's a Mets guy," Johnny said going back to his office. He picked up three folders and some invoices before coming back out.

"McKenna! You deliver that fax machine to what's her face on Water Street?"

"She said it was the wrong one, I brought it back up to sales."

"Fuckin' twat. I'll have Habib take care of it over the weekend."

"You comin' for a taste?"

"Yea. Where?"

"We go to Gilbride's on Forty-Seventh. I'm actually surprised I haven't seen you in there."

"Yea, sure I'll meet ya's there."

"What ya mean meet us there? You too good to walk with us?"

"I got twenty minutes left."

"I got ya here at five-thirty. Ralphy Boy what you got?"

"I got Gilbride-thirty."

"Let's go, kid."

Gilbride's was much like any of the Irish owned Irish operated pubs in the city with the exception of the two facts that it would become my first local, and it was a Johnny staple. A thick shot of Jameson and a bottle of Bud met him at his seat. Later I would notice that every single time Johnny acted smooth with a sincere "thank you" to the gesture but watching him time upon time, his first sips, there was pride and entitlement in his eyes.

One From The Ice

The bathroom was downstairs; the bar was forty feet, cherry stained. On Fridays we'd stay until 4:00am, sometimes later if we ate properly and stayed in good enough shape. On weekdays, usually Mondays and Thursdays, Johnny would take the crew out, but no matter how bad of shape we were in the previous night, everyone was expected the next day on time ready for a full day's nonsense. There had been a rumor that sometimes John would return back to Gilbride's for more after everyone had gone; later I would find that he had done so only a handful of times.

Our friendship had really begun when I met him on a Saturday night in November at Gilbride's. We were to meet there first before going to a house party that one of Checkmate's vice presidents would throw every year at his townhouse in Brooklyn. Why Johnny invited me, I did not know.

It was wet outside. The traffic was thick. I remember thinking that Saturday nights were born in New York, their feeling, and their dress, how we act in them. I looked good cursing the puddles, thirsty for some courage, as I was very insecure about meeting anyone in the company above John; I was a nobody.

As I walked in I saw John was already there. He heard the door open, glanced up and then away as if he had been waiting for no one. I slapped his back, he stuck out a firm hand, and I had a bottle of Bud and a shot of Jameson waiting. He raised his glass, "Good luck kid," he said.

"I can't wait for baseball," I said on the next beer.

"Yea, fuckin' Jets are done. What are you Giants?"

"Nah. I follow football, I have no team though. I mean, I know football."

"No team? You're not one of these fantasy fags are you?"

"No, of course not."

"Where'd Joe Willie play college?"

"'Bama."

"What number did Al Toon wear?"

"Eighty-Eight."

Johnny paused, and I ordered two more shots. I recognized the barman but had never been introduced. He had just stepped onto his shift. I knew he was from the Bronx; I also knew that he and Johnny were friends. He was burly with thick black hair, a permanent five o'clock shadow that I admired. His voice was as burley as his figure. He knew ninety percent of the people that walked through the door.

"Billy Force, say hello to one of my best guys, Jimmy McKenna."

One From The Ice

"What ya say, Jimmy?"

"Hi ya doin, Billy."

"Where ya from, Jimmy?"

"Nutley."

"Jersey yea? You're probably Yankees then, no?"

"Yea."

"Ah, that's all right, you seem like a decent guy," he said winking at Johnny, setting up two more shots.

"Jimmy here says he knows football. I'm over here seein' just how much of that is true."

"Football huh?" Billy paused rubbing the scruff on his chin, putting out his hand to shake a couple's hand in from St. Louis that he had met two nights ago.

"Ah…ok, I heard this from my man 'Small Bobby' the other day. What running back tandem made up the 'Pony Express?' One of 'em's a hall of famer. Gimme the college, too."

"Askin' me?" I asked sipping.

"I'm askin'."

"Dickerson was the hall of famer…" I paused scratching my nose. "Craig James was his running back at SMU."

Billy poured two more shots and knocked the wood twice, smiling wryly as he walked away. Johnny and I toasted. A thick buzz was settling in. I could read it on his face over the slight crowd noise and the unobtrusive background chimes of glass to glass, glass to wood, glass digging out ice.

Johnny began to get up and slid a five over to me. "Do me a favor kid, play some music, I gotta piss."

I knew what to do standing in front of a jukebox. The red and the green and the orange rotating their colors on my face, no pressure, no one caring on a very early Saturday night, uncomplicated with the absence of women. I had my apartment, the job, now seemingly the respect of Johnny, perhaps this guy Billy. Plenty of cash for a good November session, and now there would be music.

I played Tom Waits songs I had never heard of but Johnny had wanted mouthing the words underneath his breath. Then he would get up in quick movements, then slow, quick again playing early Rod Stewart, his favorite *The Killing Of Georgie* parts one and two. We had forgotten about the party in Brooklyn, Johnny lighting up his Reds talking about baseball, ex-girls, great and really bad sex.

One From The Ice

"We're cut from the same cloth, you and I. What'd you doin' for Christmas? If you're not doin' nothing you should come to my parents'. I mix up manhattans for my ole man and me.... Ma puts on a spread…it's nice. You should come."

"One from the ice, Johnny?"

"One from the ice Billy, please."

There were many Saturdays in almost the exact same vein that followed. Sometimes there would be Tuesdays and Mondays. At the job, I became Johnny's guy with more responsibility and as much bump in my check as he could swing. With that also came the clear window to the politics of Checkmate. Johnny said that we were doing more business than ever before with almost a third less of the manpower to which every other day would cause him to shrug and say, "What the fuck else is new?" On the other days "Tits" the fan would get thrown onto the dock, or in the trash, and the poor girl was not looking so hot with one of her blades duct taped to the rest of her, her neck struggling to go left to right.

This went on for six months with Johnny and I seeing more and more of Billy Force. By this time I remember cutting back on the Jameson. Johnny more than made up for my slack. He seemed to separate 4:00am last calls and 7:00am roll calls at work with no seepage of one into the other. Little by little, seemingly in five minute increments spread over weeks, being late for him became more and more of a problem, nobody to give the guys direction either coming in or going out. When he did show twenty minutes behind, he acted as though he had been fighting with upper management, his mood volatile, Jameson and Bud streaming out his pours, invoices strewn in chaos far past what little organization had previously existed. The afternoon chatter with the crew was hardly about sports or women, but the stories of the bar. What Billy said or did to whom the night before, who was going to have to wait until the next day for their order or pick up so we could get to Gilbride's earlier.

What little relationship he ever said he had with a long time girl, whom I never saw, Stacey, he said one day had ended. We were on the dock watching the UPS rig back in, the rear warning noise echoing off the walls, Johnny looking at his clipboard. When we yelled to the driver that he was lined up, he put the rig into gear, and turned off the engine. Johnny looked up lazily, his blue eyes coming right through his glasses as if they were not on his face.

"So…Stacey's gone. Four years. What the fuck ya' gonna do?" he sighed and moved ahead to greet the driver coming up the stairs. I saw in his face maybe the last thing that was holding him together, gone. I saw that same look in my grandfather's face when he finally

One From The Ice

comprehended that my grandmother was dead and was not coming back. In my mind I questioned if she left because of his drinking or was he drinking because she was gone? What the hell did I know, I decided, as lifted up the door of the trailer and got ready to invoice the load.

Shortly after that instance Johnny began sleeping on my futon three nights a week. I asked once if he just wanted to make it permanent figuring he needed a place to stay, and I could have used the relief on the rent. He said nothing at first, then coming out of the bathroom he caught me in the hallway and told me no, but thanked me just the same, and that it meant a lot to him that I offered. He said that he was meant to get a one bedroom through the company around the corner on Eleventh Ave, and that Gail in accounting was processing the last of the paperwork. A week and a half later, he moved into the new place on Eleventh.

Shortly after his moving in we were putting in some of our usual hours at Gilbride's at our usual seats just inside the door. Finishing a beer Johnny looked up at the end of a breath and said, "I gotta pull my head outta my ass," and left slapping me on the back.

He did. For six months Johnny ran Checkmate shipping and receiving better than I saw him when I started. With a new group of sound guys, on time, he implemented changes with new rules that he did not force, but rather gradually worked in, then adhered to them. The gray area he shifted and lived in became more black and white. Even the Gilbride's activities were kept to a strict Thursday, Friday affair, some weeks not even. Occasionally he and I would meet privately for a Saturday session.

He would start telling me about her early on if he felt that way. Then maybe relating a small story or pointing out something Stacey liked or did not, or even hated. Later on the process would repeat itself and so would John. I would slap him on the shoulder and silently flag Billy for interference, which always came with another round.

I had other friends in the past that would do the same things in similar ways; I left them in Jersey. John was different in the fact that I learned from him, and he was smarter, quicker than I was. He saw and felt things coming and going. He would choose to act or not, to be affected or not. He never would shy away from what he was, or what he did. If he thought you deserved an explanation he would give it to you quietly, privately, sincerely. If he thought the other way he told you quickly to "go and fuck yourself." He never was comfortable with a compliment, never listened to anybody who tried to show him how talented he was including me, and in hindsight, I felt I had a decent feeling of how his lovely Stacey must have felt and perhaps a bit of an idea of what had transpired between the walls of their old apartment.

One From The Ice

As I came to friend Billy Force, I learned that he and John were quite similar. Billy was much more comfortable with people, seemingly more adjusted socially, though I did not know him as well as I had come to know John. I recognized their almost identical backgrounds, their demons that would show their faces from their shadows from time to time, their ability to be completely truthful, wink, and simultaneously be completely full of shit. Generous, loyal to whom they chose to be.

I recall the two weeks Pat Raymond was not himself, spending quite a bit of time running "short" errands that were indeed short, but growing by the day. Johnny knew he was going to have to let him go so he scheduled me to take over Paddy's routes with some extra overtime. He knew Paddy could use a severance before Christmas, I agreed, so John arranged to have those overtime hours go into an envelope which made it easier on everyone and just a touch more palatable for John to let a good man go while looking him in the eye. There was a lot of Jameson poured that night.

No matter what he was feeling, pain mostly with bouts of happiness, Johnny's sandpaper wit would do tough situations at least a breath to look around, dually serving its purpose as a catharsis for him as well as a screening for the people he would let in. Through his irascibilities and all his uneven beliefs, beyond the exterior of Head of

Shipping and Receiving for Checkmate Office Supplies, which he used very much as a shield, John kept it all hidden with eloquence to heinous extremities, as if it were all a series of murders he had been committing his whole life.

He introduced me to a drinker's life from which I spent years recovering. He introduced me to Fitzgerald by throwing a copy of *This Side Of Paradise* at my head. Continually quoting masters in poignant situations, a boss came down and cut John a deep one, and when he left John stood out smiling in front of his office calmly saying "the bell tolls for thee." Later on that night at Gilbride's I asked him what he meant. He grunted and brought in a copy of *For Whom The Bell Tolls* the next day. After he finished *Cannery Row* he handed it to me saying, " I hated that piece of shit *Grapes of Wrath*, but you should read this one."

Countless times we took it home from Gilbride's, sometimes with Billy Force throwing on Neil Young in the fall, Jethro Tull in the winter, more times than not passing out to *Barfly* or *Goodfellas*, surrounded by dead soldiers of Bud, Amstel, Heineken, half eaten sandwiches the deli delivered, the city itself and our mutual love for it. Crossing Ninth Avenue to crawl the bars around the Kitchen, the lights forcing our shadows to intertwine almost shapeless with the concrete and glass of the storefronts, with thick buzzes and heavy pockets, not thinking because it

One From The Ice

was more than enough for us, and I truly felt Johnny was my brother and envisioned knowing him for the rest of my life.

But as the drink tends to fool, it fooled Johnny into thinking that his pride in achievement should rest solely on the docks of Checkmate Office Supply. I would tell him from time to time that he should teach. He laughed or told me to shut the fuck up, always smiling afterward. When moments would become softer amongst the flow of conversation I tried to tell John what I saw, what I thought he was, what he had to offer giving him examples that maybe would roll into possibilities. With a Jameson slur and Budweiser eyes he would twist his hand as if it were crippled and say, "Jimmy we're cut from the same cloth, I got no talent. Books, a job, and you...that's what I got." Always on the verge of trying to find in himself just what I was talking about, I could see him thinking about it. It took the course of one April for John to let go.

Resorting to his days when Stacey had left, puking into the big blue dumpsters to sweat it out and perhaps somewhat be functional for the job. Slipping past upper management, creating more and more absurd routes and tasks for the drivers and me, back to smudging invoices, late morning or afternoon naps sometimes in plain sight in the office, sometimes continuing them in the recycling room in makeshift hammocks amongst the squeals of rats and the smell of piss both stale or fresh.

At some point Johnny had been introduced to cocaine. My suspicions had been cemented when Billy Force took me aside when Johnny was in the can. I knew Billy partied some and thus took it more seriously when he pulled me aside for a word.

"Jimmy Boy, I'm not tryin to tell tales, a man does what a man does, it's just that Johnny's our man, and he listens to you. You gotta step in somehow, like before, he's getting nuts again." It was too late that evening; we both were too in the bag. I planned to get him later in the week, preferably early in the crawl.

The following Thursday Johnny went to town on me on Eighth Avenue and 44th Street. We were on our way to the first stop on 46th Street arguing once again who the better short stop was, Ordonez or Vizquel. My mind was on my approach to getting his head to come around to maybe something more when the wind was knocked out of me quickly and unexpected. I then remember getting turned around and feeling similar pain in my ribs, then something hitting me in my nose, my eyes blurring orange, white as I fell. The sidewalk danced up and down, up and down. When my breath started to return slightly, I smelled a sulphur scent that caused me to puke. I remembered a hand on my right thigh, then inside my pocket along with warm liquid by my ear and in my hair.

One From The Ice

I came to with my brother beside me at St. Claire's. He asked what had happened along with the two cops who were also there. I said I got jumped, told them where it hurt. They asked whom I was with; I said I was alone, on my way to meet Johnny. My brother asked where Johnny was. I said I didn't know. The cops said there was a Korean guy who saw a short white kid running towards Ninth Avenue with bloody hands and blood on the side of his face. I shook my head. They asked if I had been in a fight recently, I said no. Any enemies they asked, I said no. They asked me again if I knew where Johnny might be, I said I didn't know.

Two weeks and I was back at Checkmate. They had given me sick leave and had offered me a position just below Johnny's, and that Johnny had not been heard or seen from. I worked a week and quit. I left midtown and took a bartending gig in New Rochelle. For two months I waited outside Gilbride's, John's apartment, and quietly outside the dock at Checkmate. I walked Tenth to Columbus Circle, Ninth to 34th, Seventh, Broadway from the West Side Highway to Fifth Avenue. Johnny hated the East Side, and if he was there I would get him sooner or later, and the same would go for Jersey. Billy Force made tracks to Boston where he got in on some points at a beer bar just outside Fenway.

After some time the anger left me. As much as I tried to hold onto it, it just went away. A while after that I got sick of taking the Seven

Train to Grand Central, transferring to the Metro North, then taking the $50.00 cab ride back to Woodside. The job was becoming too lucrative to quit. As much as it pained me, I moved out of Woodside to an apartment two blocks from the bar in New Rochelle, just off of Municipal Marina and not long into the summer, found myself saving for my first boat.

With my confidence growing in bartending, I got two more shifts and the owner Rory's trust. Most of how I ran the shift I imitated from Billy Force, and most of how I cut corners for the house's benefits I learned from Johnny.

A full year went bringing in fall's cool replenishments. I would venture into the city less and less, and when I did, the places I would go were below Fourteenth Street, sometimes a happy hour around the Financial District, only really stopping in midtown for a quick pint and a piss. Never back to Gilbride's.

At Rory's I would sometimes end with a Budweiser and a shot of Jameson listening to *The Killing Of Georgie I & II* while I sat alone feeling the scar at the top of my head, looking out at the quiet shifts and slides of the boats faintly highlighted by the orange overhead lamps, sometimes with the accompaniment of the moon.

On a September morning, three years later, at 11:00am I read John's obituary. I found it even stranger; I never read things of that

One From The Ice

nature, but I happened to glance over them that day, as if I had been meant to. I read it three times, the only thing that would come to mind was his mother, her hard Irish face, soft demeanor, and the time we met briefly on a fall afternoon just outside the dock of Checkmate Office Supply.

ScW

Sean Welsh was born and raised in Cleveland, Ohio in the seventies and eighties. Upon moving to New York City, Sean started bartending and has continued to do so for over 10 years. In 2003 he co-founded *The Goodluck and All the Best*, a quarterly literary journal which was distributed in NYC bars for two years. He watches 162 regular season Yankee games per year and is always pulling for them in the post-season. Sean Welsh continues to live and write in New York City.

Made in the USA
Middletown, DE
18 July 2017